CRESTWOOD HILLS
The Chronicle of a Modern Utopia

Cory Buckner

ACP
ANGEL CITY PRESS

In memory of my late husband, Nick Roberts

Contents

MHA Model 111X · *Overleaf:* Schneidman House and owner, Kristin MacDowell

Introduction

Hidden away in Los Angeles in a hillside neighborhood called Brentwood, perched high above what is now the 405 freeway linking the north and south of America's most populous state, is Crestwood Hills, the prototype for California modern living, an innovative concept with Utopian ideals—a blueprint for creating communities where very real people can live in extraordinary homes on their very real incomes. For this reason alone, Crestwood Hills would hold an important place in the history of twentieth century architecture and residential development—but there is so much more to its story.

Established in 1946, Crestwood Hills, formerly Mutual Housing Association (MHA), marks the first time that the full palette of modernist spatial and material invention was used on a large-scale cooperative housing development in Southern California. The exploratory invention brought to the region by architects Richard Neutra, Rudolph Schindler, and Frank Lloyd Wright, and continued by the next generation of Gregory Ain, Harwell Harris, and Thornton Abell, was confined to single-family residences, small multi-family projects, and commercial buildings. Clarence S. Stein and Henry Wright's Baldwin Hills Village (which was later known as Village Green), and other garden apartments of the 1930s and 1940s, and Neutra's Channel Heights Housing of 1941 through 1943, addressed large multi-family dwellings in a modernist language. MHA is one of the few fulfillments of the Bauhaus dream introduced in the International Exhibition of Modern Architecture at the Museum of Modern Art in 1932. Bringing good design and economical construction to moderate-income housing on a large scale, MHA was the clear forerunner of the celebrated modernist housing projects of the 1960s.

Crestwood Hills is the only successful large-scale modern housing cooperative in the West. Despite virulent opposition from local authorities all the way up to the Federal government, Crestwood Hills was built as conceived: people lived in architecturally significant structures, and people continue to live in those homes in the twenty-first century. Its founders' experience with cooperatives in Canada and the United States, their social idealism, and the charismatic leadership of its founders

Opposite: Mutual Housing Association model number 301, photographed by Julius Shulman in 1950

Architects

Whitney R. Smith

A. Quincy Jones

Garret Eckbo

We have chosen some of the foremost thinkers in the field of modern architecture to design the entire project. They are: Whitney R. Smith and A. Quincy Jones, Architects; Edgardo Contini, Engineer; and Garret Eckbo, landscape architect, who is assisting in the site-planning.

Edgardo Contini

From an early brochure for Mutual Housing Association, Inc.

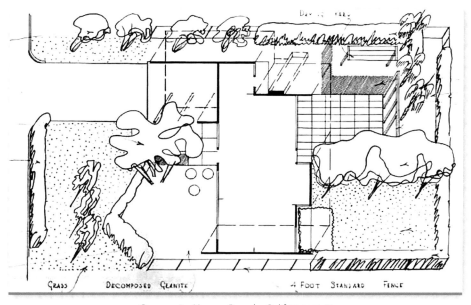

Community Homes, Reseda, Calif. 1947–1948

create a fascinating narrative of progressive politics, social utopianism, and tough lobbying that enabled the group to successfully navigate the requirements of the neighborhood, the City of Los Angeles, and the Federal Housing Administration. Unlike other socially progressive projects of the time such as the Community Homes, designed by Ain, Johnson, and Day (an unrealized project intended for construction in Reseda, California), and Ladera in the foothills above Stanford University in Northern California, the MHA was able to build a sustainable, socially responsible neighborhood. Though ultimately stripped of some of its most controversial social features and with far fewer houses than originally planned, this landmark community remains a tribute to the people who envisioned it.

Los Angeles held special appeal to the many servicemen who had passed through the area during World War II. They returned to what looked like paradise only to find a desperate lack of housing; demobilized servicemen and their families were sleeping in tents and Quonset hut camps in the city parks. The MHA started as a way for four returning veterans, all studio musicians, to build houses for their families and share a common swimming pool. As the word spread among the musicians' friends, there were soon twenty-five families interested, and the membership quickly grew to one hundred. The four realized they had started a movement when, after placing an ad in the *Hollywood Citizen-News*, they had five hundred people interested. The project had quickly grown to a community, which was

to include not only housing, but also amenities to serve the group as a whole. MHA was to become the largest cooperative housing development attempted in postwar California.

After interviewing such renowned architects as Richard Neutra, Lloyd Wright, Douglas Honnold, and John Lautner, the MHA selected architects Whitney R. Smith and A. Quincy Jones and structural engineer Edgardo Contini. As the last selected, Contini contributed his skill at engineering and his love of hillside construction. The three created a design body known as the "joint venture" to plan the community and design the houses.

Like other architects who had flocked to Los Angeles after the war, energized by the desperate need for housing and bringing experimental ideas based on new materials resulting from the war effort, the MHA team was determined to design innovative structures that could be erected simply and cheaply and that reflected the politically progressive visions of the founding members. According to a very early brochure presented to prospective members,

> The entire project will be designed for living instead of for speculation. This is not an emergency housing project but is to be carefully designed and built in accordance with a long-range plan. Planning, purchasing, building, and details of the houses, will be discussed by the membership. We are planning community facilities to include nursery schools, swimming pools, tennis courts, a cooperative market, etc. The aim is an integrated community designed to secure the best in living for minimum of cost.

Originally 350 lots were carved into the eight-hundred-acre hillside parcel purchased by the Association. The idea was to build the small and affordable houses on the slopes of the property, which would leave the best flat land for the communal facilities. Community members could select from twenty-eight house plans with each member being assigned a number based on the date of membership. Of the 350 lots, approximately eighty-five were built out using the MHA designs; more than two hundred houses were designed by other architects adhering to design guidelines, which are still enforced today. The Bel Air fire of 1961 destroyed forty-nine of the homes, and many more have been remodeled beyond recognition. At this writing, only forty-seven of the remaining homes are representative of their original design.

Shortly after a Malibu brush fire destroyed the house my late husband, Nick Roberts, and I designed and built, we started the search for a replacement home in Los Angeles. Several years before the

Opposite: Channel Heights Housing, 1941–1942, Richard Neutra

fire, I had been hired to remodel two of the original houses in Crestwood Hills. The transparency, structural elegance, and soaring spaces of the MHA houses intrigued me, and the feeling of a distinct, involved community convinced both of us that this was an area where we could be happy living.

Not long after we bought our first house in Crestwood Hills—the Haas House, an original MHA house—our friend Donna Vaccarino introduced me to Elaine Sewell Jones, the widow of A. Quincy Jones, who showed me the archive of her husband's work. I proposed to Elaine that I write a book on Jones's work. She agreed, and the result was a publication by Phaidon Press in 2002, *A. Quincy Jones,* which included a brief history of the Mutual Housing Association.

Nick and I became increasingly distressed at the rate at which the remaining MHA houses were being demolished or remodeled beyond recognition. In 1994, the properties were selling for little more than the value of the land. While there was an Architecture Committee in place during the development, there were worrisome violations of the original Architectural Guidelines. In hopes of starting a preservation movement, Nick and I invited all the owners of the original MHA houses to a meeting to discuss working together to establish a Historic Preservation Overlay Zone (HPOZ). The negative reaction to this idea took

us both by complete surprise. Owners, including one of the founding members, were fearful of losing property value by establishing an HPOZ. Only a handful of homeowners had any interest in keeping the integrity of the houses and the neighborhood.

After the meeting, we proposed an alternate strategy to the few homeowners dedicated to preservation: I would present applications for Historic-Cultural Monument status to the Los Angeles Cultural Heritage Commission for each house individually. Our first attempt at listing five of the houses was fraught with opposition. Only a few on the Commission felt there was any merit in giving monument status to something just fifty years old. After weeks of concentrated effort, obtaining letters from photographer Julius Shulman, Elaine Sewell Jones, and neighbor and Councilman Marvin Braude, we were able to get four of the five houses declared Historic-Cultural Monuments by the City of Los Angeles. Every two years after that, I presented another four or five houses until fifteen were declared Historic-Cultural Monuments. Fortunately, almost all new homeowners appreciate the significance of their houses and take over the applications themselves. By 2015, eighteen of the remaining forty-seven houses were declared Historic-Cultural Monuments.

Opposite: The Haas House, MHA Model 111X

PART ONE

Chapter One

Formation

It was 1946 and they were young, talented, and educated. During the day the four men earned their keep as studio musicians at Paramount. At night and over the weekends they dreamed of living in an ideal community. Within months they had convinced five hundred families to share their dream, providing the resources to buy eight hundred acres of what would soon become Brentwood, the prestigious Los Angeles neighborhood. They engaged a team of similarly young and idealistic architects and engineers; a few years later they started building Crestwood Hills.

They quickly learned that creating a new community was a massive undertaking. The first step, for instance, turned out to be the largest earth-moving project that had ever been attempted west of the Mississippi. When the work began, no one, not the leaders of the fledgling community nor the designers, knew exactly what they were doing. Nor did they have any idea what other obstacles they would face.

McCarthyism was on the rise, a war with Korea was inflating the costs of building materials, racism was as always a potent factor in real estate,

and modernist houses were anathema to banks and building departments. Those were realities. The four idealists—Jules Salkin, Gene Komer, Leonard Krupnick, and Ray Siegel—were determined to employ modernist architecture to build a nonprofit, cooperatively built and operated, progressive, interracial enclave. They wanted to create a utopia.

World War II and its aftermath had drawn millions of new residents to California. Thousands had moved to work at the state's wartime aircraft factories, and servicemen had discovered the attraction of California during their training for the Pacific theater. After the war, the aircraft industry, universities, and the movie industry attracted many veterans who dreamed of starting a new life in an area with mild weather, seemingly endless employment opportunities, and breathtaking beauty. The result was an increase in the state's population from 6.91 million in 1940 to 10.59 million in 1950, and an acute housing shortage.

Many families were temporarily housed in makeshift structures such as the Roger Young Village in Griffith Park, which consisted of 750 corrugated steel Quonset huts. The structures were

Opposite: Roger Young Village in Griffith Park · *Overleaf:* Grading in progress for Mutual Housing Association

intended to house 1,500 families; at its peak, more than five thousand people lived there. Others settled for poorly constructed developer homes that spread across the San Fernando Valley and other rapidly expanding tract developments. Developers gave little thought to providing any amenities for the buyers of their houses.

In 1946, three of the idealists met one evening to discuss the possibility of combining their resources to purchase an acre of land. They envisioned building a house at each of the four corners of the property with a shared swimming pool and play area in the center. The inspiration of this scheme came from Jules Salkin who had seen a similar plan, Suntop Homes, on the drafting boards at Frank Lloyd Wright's Taliesin. Salkin played violin during the summers of 1938 and 1939 at Taliesin. Ray Siegel, Leonard Krupnick, and Salkin had met in Brazil while touring with the All-American Youth Orchestra, and later played together in the Indianapolis Philharmonic prior to the war. As they searched for a fourth member, word spread among their friends. Gene Komer, a trumpet player and fellow serviceman with Siegel, completed the necessary foursome. Shortly after Komer joined, twenty-five people—many of them professionals, including several professors from

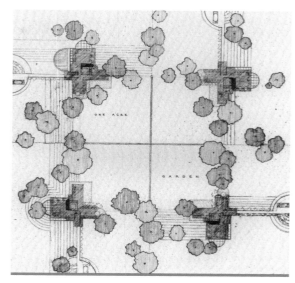

Top: Suntop Homes • *Bottom*: Ray Siegel

Opposite: Jules Salkin in Brazil

The Rochdale store with all employees, 1910

nearby UCLA—agreed to combine their resources, expanding the project from the original one-acre plan.

The group incorporated in August of 1946 as the Mutual Housing Association (MHA), a non-profit cooperative allied with the International Cooperative Association (ICA). The ICA was developed based on the Rochdale Principles of the Rochdale Society of Equitable Pioneers, a group of weavers in Rochdale, England. In 1844, with the advent of the Industrial Revolution and in conjunction with firings after a weaver's strike, many skilled workers were forced into poverty. With members pooling 140 British pounds, the group organized an open cooperative store selling food products they could not otherwise afford.

The earliest example of a cooperative organization in the United States was started by none other than Benjamin Franklin. The Philadelphia Contributionship, the first successful fire insurance company in the colonies, was formed with his fellow volunteer firefighters in 1752. The company formed as a mutual insurance company, one in which policyholders agreed to make equal payments to the Contributionship, which would be used to pay for losses any member would sustain through fire to their property. Later, in the U.S., rural electric co-ops, credit unions, and agricultural (including housing) co-ops were founded to meet the needs of populations, particularly rural communities, which did not attract investment or where goods and services were only otherwise available at unfair prices.

One of the founding four members of the MHA, Leonard Krupnick, was raised on a commune in Wisconsin. He had firsthand knowledge of cooperative communities around the world, information essential to the formation of a successful housing cooperative. Prior to forming the MHA, he had ten years experience in the cooperative movement, serving as president of a grocery co-op in Chicago and then as a member of two other

MHA site shortly after purchase, 1947

and association could sustain only four hundred.

Bell's original vision was to turn the Santa Monica Mountains into prestigious properties, the same approach he took in Bel Air. Jules Salkin knew that Bell would be skeptical about selling land to a cooperative with a large Jewish membership, since wealthy and conservative households would surround the community. Salkin's wife's uncle, a wealthy developer, fronted the purchase of the acreage on behalf of the cooperative for four hundred thousand dollars, a per-acre cost of five

hundred dollars. The MHA members held most of the same principles in common, but their progressive attitude was an anomaly in the well-heeled neighborhoods that surrounded them.

MHA wasn't the first cooperative housing venture for many of the members. With strong socialist beliefs, early members like Nora Weckler, a psychologist, and her husband, Joseph, an anthropologist, had hoped to join an earlier cooperative, Community Homes, that architect Gregory Ain designed in Reseda. When that venture fell apart, the Wecklers sought out "the cooperative started by four musicians." The cooperative aspect was very important to Nora, who had been raised in Toronto by socialist parents who had supported MP J.S. Woodsworth of the Cooperative Commonwealth Federation, a political party established to protect the interests of farmers and workers through economic co-operation, socialization of the economy, and political reform. A way of life committed to working together as a community was an important aspect to the Wecklers' participation; Nora would later become the founding president of the nursery school.

Joseph Meyerson, an attorney and CPA, purchased an MHA share. He had been chairman of the board serving pro bono on the Twin Pines Consumer Co-op of Santa Monica, which functioned until the 1970s. Another early member, Max Silver, was the organizational secretary of the Los Angeles County Communist Party from the late 1930s through the mid-1940s and later called before the House Committee on Un-American Activities.

These progressive beliefs were soon put to a test. Hermann Schott, a successful biochemist, lived with his wife, Vida, on lower Tigertail Road just outside the MHA community. Vida had started the first cooperative nursery school in the Los Angeles area, located in Santa Monica. As friends of Philip and Leah Lovell, who had hired Rudolph Schindler to build their Lovell Beach House and Richard Neutra to build the Lovell Health House near Griffith Park, the Schotts had developed a sophisticated eye for architecture.

Several of Schott's Hollywood musician friends joined the MHA and convinced him to consider investing in the endeavor. Schott, of German descent and older than the average MHA member, had been aware of the currency devaluation in Germany after World War I and feared something similar happening in the United States. He happily sold his large house on Tigertail and purchased a share of the Mutual Housing Association. Schott immediately became active in the community and formed the Crestwood Hills Credit Union in 1947, serving as both its president and treasurer at various times. Only residents of Crestwood Hills could join the credit union, but they could remain members if they moved away from the community.

Prior to his participation in MHA, Schott selected acreage outside of Crestwood Hills on Tigertail Road at Bonhill Road and constructed a large modern house designed by Rolf Sklare. Actor Henry Fonda and his family lived across from the Schotts, and Mrs. Fonda called Hermann Schott one day, inquiring about the new MHA development. According to Schott, he said something about letting in people of other races, and that this

Site Plan

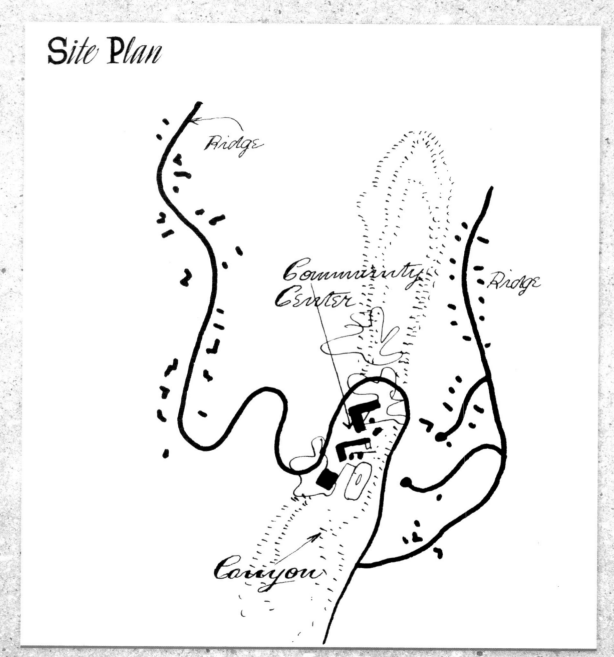

Proposed house layout for Crestwood Hills. The community center and park are at the center.

SITE PLAN

LADERA
PENINSULA HOUSING ASSOCIATION

Site plan for the Ladera cooperative housing project in Northern California

was a good thing. Upset about his statement, Mrs. Fonda said she would talk to the powers that be who ran the Residential Land Corporation. Very soon after, the sales agency made race restrictions a condition of sale; the Federal Housing Administration (FHA) already had similar restrictions nationwide. Since the MHA had a contract to purchase the property, an emergency meeting was held at the Roosevelt Hotel where the issue was debated. At the time, Albert Nasaki, an art director at Paramount, and his wife were the only minority members of the MHA. Several of the dedicated members withdrew on principle before the vote was taken to comply with the FHA race restrictions. Salkin knew the issue would not be enforced by the membership, and the Supreme Court would be ruling on the matter of racially restrictive covenants in the very near future. The vote was taken to continue with the purchase and to meet the demands of the Residential Land Corporation to restrict blacks and Chinese from purchasing land; the Nasakis were asked to withdraw their membership. The Wecklers withdrew, but immediately rejoined as soon as the Supreme Court's 1948 Shelley v. Kraemer judgment made exclusionary covenants unconstitutional under the Fourteenth Amendment and therefore legally unenforceable.

Another cooperative community in Northern California had been founded a few years too early to survive the conflict created by the FHA racial restrictions. In 1944, the Peninsula Housing Association (PHA) formed with 150 members and purchased 260 acres of gently rolling terrain near Palo Alto and Stanford University. The members chose the name Ladera for the community after considering New Rochdale. Early members included author Wallace Stegner and inventor Sigurd Varian, who was raised near San Luis Obispo in a religious cooperative called Halcyon. Garrett Eckbo, who would be part of the MHA team a few years later, designed the layout for the new Ladera community. Due to financial difficulties after the members refused to place restrictive covenants on the deeds, the PHA failed after constructing just a handful of houses. The land was sold to a developer.

The purpose of the MHA was to organize an integrated community with architectural control and cooperative principles. It became a corporation established for the sole purpose of developing and selling the individual lots to the members. The association would be dissolved at the end of the land development and distribution of parcels, necessitating the need for a new name for the community. A "name the project" contest ran in the community bulletin with a deadline of May 1, 1947; the social committee announced the winning name: Crestwood Hills.

CREATING AN UNUSUAL COMMUNITY

Making plans for the community several hundred families will build are: seated (from left) architects Whitney R. Smith, Douglas Honnold, and A. Quincy Jones. Standing (from left) are John Lautner, an associate of Honnold; Francis Lockwood, architect; Garrett Eckbo, landscape designer, and Edgardo Contini, engineer. (Citizen-News photo).

CHAPTER TWO

Architecture

Los Angeles attracted the best and brightest architects; they saw an opportunity to build in a mild climate with lightweight materials developed during the war effort. In large part, this was thanks to the efforts of John Entenza, the editor of *Arts and Architecture* magazine. Not only did Entenza and his magazine introduce the most modern and efficient architectural design practices to Southern California and beyond, it sponsored the famed Case Study House program begun in 1945. Case Study Houses, which were meant to be affordable homes for the typical middle-class family, showcased several major innovations that became standard in popular house design. They included open floor plans with minimal internal walls to allow for flexible use and the integration of indoor/outdoor living through the use of sliding glass doors. *Arts & Architecture* published all thirty-six Case Study Houses designs; of those, twenty-four were built for clients.

As well as being politically progressive, the members of the Mutual Housing Association wished to express their advanced outlook through modern architectural design. The design committee interviewed Richard Neutra, Lloyd Wright, and John Lautner, among others. According to early member Gerald Tannen, the members even considered Frank Lloyd Wright, since some of them were familiar with the nearby Sturges House. Neutra presented a proposal and asked for a ten-thousand-dollar retainer for the preliminary designs, a fee the committee felt was too high, disappointing many of the members.

Because of Jules Salkin's stay in Taliesin, he brought a unique sophisticated knowledge of architecture and became a proponent of using modern, economical design in the MHA development. While Salkin was at Taliesin, the 1934 model for Broadacre City was on display in the living room, showcasing Wright's idea of a vast low-density sprawling city of privately owned homes and publicly owned facilities. Broadacre City had a variety of building types and social and cultural activities designed for a very specific population. In one corner of the otherwise flat twelve-foot by twelve-foot model, the contours change into hillside

Opposite: Hollywood Citizen-News, Second Section, Saturday Dec. 28, 1946

Top: Broadacre City model with Frank Lloyd Wright and apprentices. · Bottom: Broadacre City Hillside House, Frank Lloyd Wright

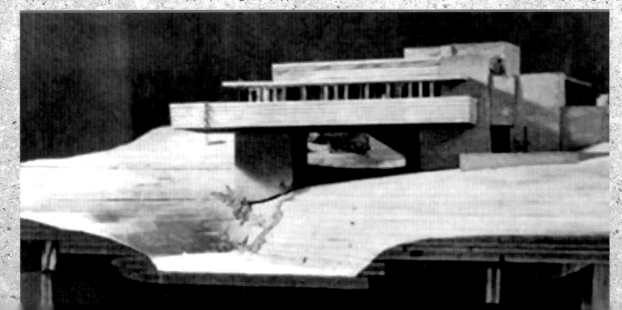

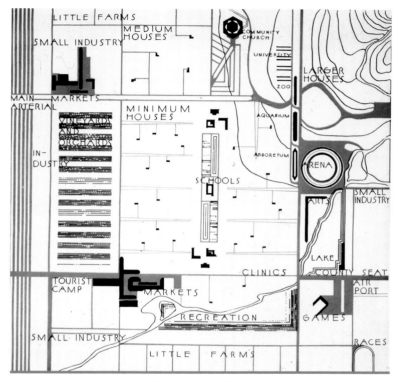

Broadacre City Plan

topography, an area designated for large houses. Many of the house designs for Broadacre City were departures from Wright's previous designs, which had been solidly positioned on masonry bases, appearing to grow upward, organically from the ground plane. The hillside houses on the Broadacre model cantilever dramatically and display horizontal ribbon windows above a horizontal form, a geometry in direct contrast to the organic nature of the hill.

Based on this Taliesin-born bias, Salkin had

initially approached former Wrightian apprentice John Lautner to discuss designing the houses for the MHA. Lautner referred him to his former boss and collaborator at the time, Douglas Honnold. Honnold was an accomplished architect, best known for having designed an inventive house for actress Dolores del Rio in Santa Monica Canyon. Honnold and Lautner had collaborated on several projects including Coffee Dan Restaurants, and the modern remodel of the Beverly Hills Athletic Club. Lautner had relocated to Los Angeles to supervise Wright's Sturges House in Brentwood, just down the street from the future MHA development. Another Taliesin apprentice, Jim Charlton, who would later play a decisive role in the MHA designs, visited Lautner at the construction site.

According to an article published in the *Hollywood Citizen-News*, December 28, 1946, the MHA design team was originally composed of architects Douglas Honnold, Whitney R. Smith, A. Quincy Jones, John Lautner, and Francis Lockwood, as well as landscape architect Garrett Eckbo and

Model of Case Study House #24 by A. Quincy Jones and Frederick E. Emmons

engineer Edgardo Contini. Jim Charlton worked for the team and produced loose, freehand colored-pencil perspective renderings of the team's vision. During the concept-design phase, Lautner had an affair with Honnold's wife, and the two architects parted ways. The distraught Honnold turned over the project to A. Quincy Jones and Whitney R. Smith. The association insisted on a third member, which resulted in the inclusion of Honnold's structural engineer Edgardo Contini, who was selected for his interest in working with hillside properties. Garrett Eckbo remained as the landscape consultant. Despite contention among

MHA members, many still wishing to hire Neutra even with his high price, the MHA architecture design team became the joint venture of Whitney R. Smith, A. Quincy Jones, and Edgardo Contini.

A. Quincy Jones, the most accomplished of the three, produced architecture consistently inventive and appropriate to the issues of his generation. In 1961, he would go on to design with his then-partner, Frederick E. Emmons, the only large tract home development for the Case Study Program, the unbuilt Case Study #24. His exploration of new building materials and construction techniques resulted in innovative approaches to

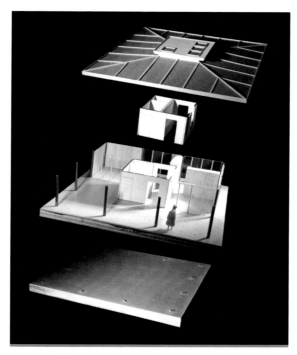

Plyluminum House, 1940, Whitney R. Smith

traditional building types. Bridging the gap between custom-built and merchant-built homes, Jones was interested in creating the dynamic architecture for the postwar, moderate-income family, the kind of architecture usually reserved for wealthy clients.

Whitney R. Smith designed two houses for the Case Study House program in 1946. Both CSH #5 and #12 were unbuilt but published with the other CSH house designs. The Smith designs are impressive in their innovation. Prior to the Case Study program, Smith experimented with plywood in his design for Plyluminun House, a project featuring movable prefabricated walls designed for flexibility in meeting client needs. His interest in modular construction and prefabrication became essential in the MHA designs, which depended on a repetitive system to curb costs of construction. Within his own private practice established in the early 1940s, Smith worked closely with Wayne R. Williams, later to become the award-winning design firm Smith and Williams; Smith brought in Williams to work the MHA project.

Engineer Edgardo Contini transitioned easily into working with Jones and Smith. He was intrigued by the undeveloped, difficult hillside the MHA had acquired and felt up to the challenge. He stated in an interview, "It looked to be fascinating work; no one knew too much about it and we were encouraged to do the best we could with the land." Contini also participated in the house designs and became an MHA member. His brother and his parents also both became members, but all eventually sold their lots without building in the community.

The concept assigned to the joint venture was unique; the eight hundred acres would consist of individual lots and public amenities to serve the community as a whole consisting of such communal facilities as a clubhouse, restaurant, medical office, preschool, and gas station. Each MHA member would own land and pick a house design from fifteen to eighteen prototypes designed by the team.

Landscape architect Garrett Eckbo, a Har-

Edgardo Contini, A. Quincy Jones, and Whitney R. Smith

vard-trained modernist, suggested keeping intact the natural elements of the upper-ridge sites and grading the lower acreage, which was much more varied, into terraced strips. The joint venture of architects and designers proposed keeping the majority of the flat, open space for the community services, keeping the residential lots small. To compensate for the small lot size, lots of differing shapes were specified at odd angles to one another. A. Quincy Jones had previously experimented with this advanced approach to tract development with a project he designed in San Diego for the developer Del Webb. The concept proved to be very successful in providing each property with ample garden areas and a sense of privacy between lots. The best flat land in the MHA project

was set aside for the clubhouse or "big room" as it was referred to, a large space intended for medical offices, the credit union, and social rooms for club meetings. A restaurant for communal dining was proposed next to the big room, adjacent to grassy areas surrounding the swimming pool. Scattered about the prime flat land at the bowl of the property were to be an open-air theater, arts-and-crafts room, tennis and badminton courts, and an area for quiet games such as horseshoes and croquet, that was to be situated closest to the preschool. In addition, a gas station and a building to house a food and dry goods market, beauty parlor, shoe repair, and laundry were proposed along the street frontage.

While some MHA members had connections

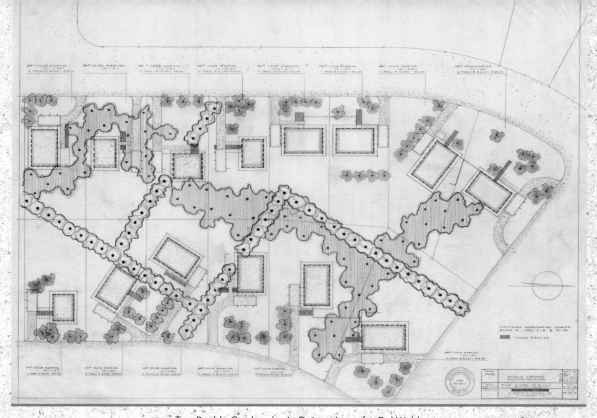

Top: Pueblo Gardens by A. Quincy Jones for Del Webb
Bottom: Site plan for houses grouped on Rochedale Lane and Bramble Lane.

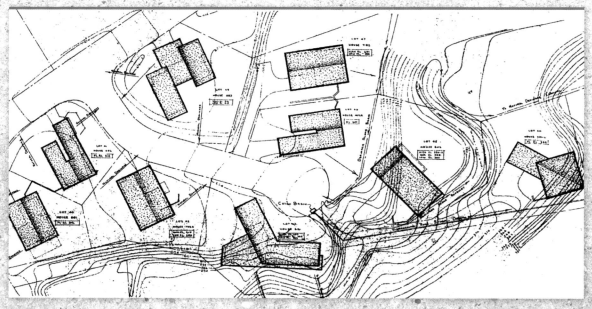

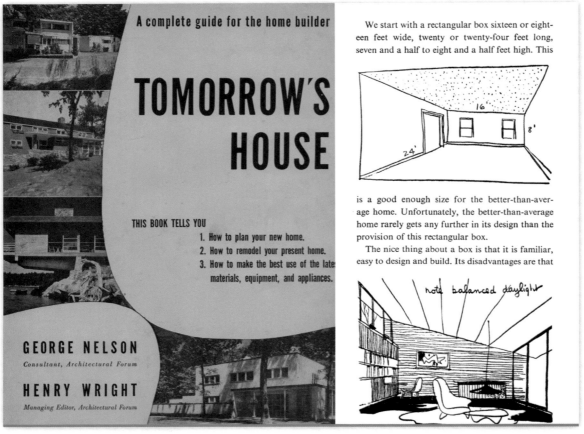

A complete guide for the home builder

TOMORROW'S HOUSE

THIS BOOK TELLS YOU

1. How to plan your new home.
2. How to remodel your present home.
3. How to make the best use of the latest materials, equipment, and appliances.

GEORGE NELSON
Consultant, Architectural Forum

HENRY WRIGHT
Managing Editor, Architectural Forum

We start with a rectangular box sixteen or eighteen feet wide, twenty or twenty-four feet long, seven and a half to eight and a half feet high. This

is a good enough size for the better-than-average home. Unfortunately, the better-than-average home rarely gets any further in its design than the provision of this rectangular box.

The nice thing about a box is that it is familiar, easy to design and build. Its disadvantages are that

note balanced daylight

Cover and page insert, *Tomorrow's House,* by Nelson and Wright • *Opposite:* Site Plan for MHA Community Services

to the art and cultural worlds of Los Angeles, few were educated in contemporary architecture. Interested members made efforts to educate other members about current architecture trends. One MHA bulletin from January of 1947 announced the purchase of a large quantity of *Tomorrow's House* by George Nelson and Henry Wright, and the classic book was made available to members, to help expand their knowledge of modern architecture for modern living. One of finest works on the topic, it contained more than two hundred pictures of interiors and exteriors by leading architects of its day and served as a primer in modern residential domestic architecture.

The architectural team presented a dozen experimental designs to the MHA architecture committee in May of 1948. The association was not quite ready for the radical new designs, and

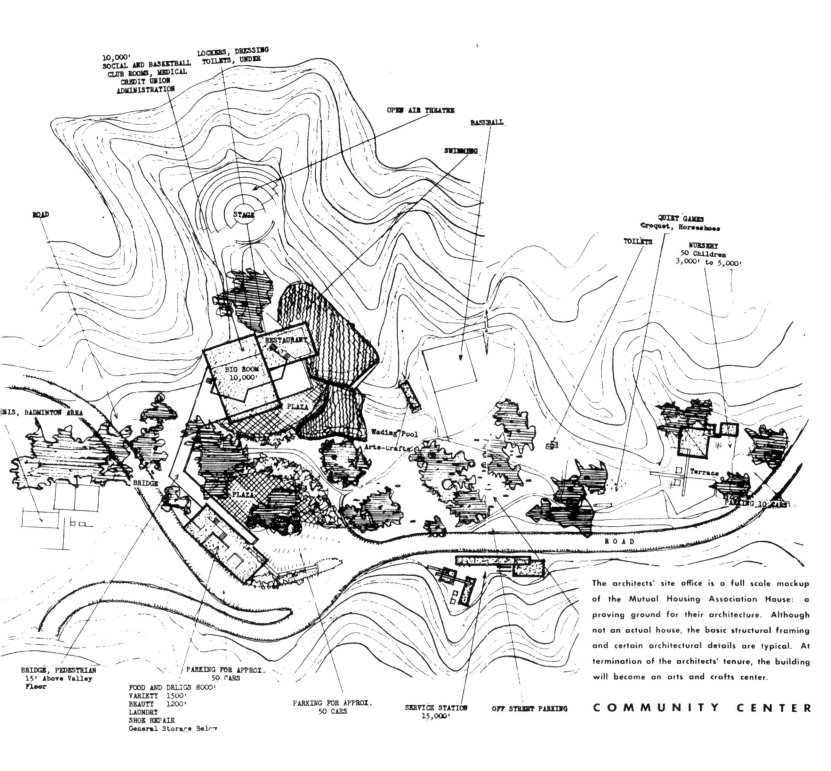

10,000'
SOCIAL AND BASKETBALL
CLUB ROOMS, MEDICAL
CREDIT UNION
ADMINISTRATION

LOCKERS, DRESSING
TOILETS, UNDER

OPEN AIR THEATRE

BASEBALL

SWIMMING

ROAD

STAGE

QUIET GAMES
Croquet, Horseshoes

TOILETS

NURSERY
50 Children
3,000' to 5,000'

RESTAURANT

BIG ROOM
10,000'

PLAZA

NIS, BADMINTON AREA

Wading Pool

Arts-Crafts

BRIDGE

Terrace

PLAZA

PARKING 10 CARS

ROAD

BRIDGE, PEDESTRIAN
15' Above Valley
Floor

PARKING FOR APPROX.
50 CARS

FOOD AND DRINKS 8000'
VARIETY   1500'
BEAUTY   1200'
LAUNDRY
SHOE REPAIR
General Storage Below

PARKING FOR APPROX.
50 CARS

SERVICE STATION
15,000'

OFF STREET PARKING

The architects' site office is a full scale mockup of the Mutual Housing Association House: a proving ground for their architecture. Although not an actual house, the basic structural framing and certain architectural details are typical. At termination of the architects' tenure, the building will become an arts and crafts center.

COMMUNITY CENTER

Top: MHA model 111 displayed in the MHA Site Office · Bottom: MHA Model 108X

Top: MHA Model 301 · Bottom: MHA Model 702

Taliesin West living room

Five Hundred
Building Bees

Robert A. Lockwood paintings

This house is Design 103 and is one of 20 styles to be built by Mutual Housing Association for 500 families in a setting of hills and woodlands.

FIVE HUNDRED FAMILIES POOLED RESOURCES IN A MUTUAL PROJECT FOR HOMES SUCH AS THIS ONE DRAMATICALLY PLACED ON A HILLSIDE TRACT NEAR BEL-AIR.

By Lee Howard

(Illustrated on Cover)

LOGROLLINGS and building bees are out of date now, but not the spirit that inspired them. Five hundred families in the Los Angeles area have banded together in a mutual housing association based on those pioneer principles of co-operation and community effort.

They have purchased an 835-acre tract west of Bel-Air and north of Brentwood which will be known as Crestwood Hills. Construction of homes in 20 different designs, each individually fitted to its site, will begin by the end of this year.

In union there is not only strength but also enthusiasm and inspiration, the originators of the project have found. The idea started in April of 1946 when the families of four musicians decided that they could pool their resources and all obtain better homes—maybe even a swimming pool—than they could individually.

So attractive were the possibilities that they soon were joined by friends who later brought in more friends. What started with four families grew in two years to include 500. Now the membership has been closed. No more families will be accepted.

Individual lots will be approximately one-quarter acre,

Concrete block and wood frame construction are shown in this covered terrace of Crestwood Hills home near Bel-Air.

From an article in *Los Angeles Times Home Magazine*, May 9, 1948

BLUEPRINT FOR
CALIFORNIA LIVING
CRESTWOOD HILLS

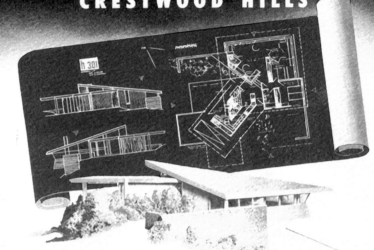

LIVE IN THE COMMUNITY OF TOMORROW...TODAY

500 MODERN HOMES — DESIGNED FOR CALIFORNIA LIVING . . . . .

Every detail has been deliberated by the architects who designed them *and by the families who will live in them.*

More than two years of planning and preparation are back of the homes in Crestwood Hills. The result: distinctive California homes, designed expressly for California living at costs that can be met by families of moderate income.

Pilot House

With the success of their second presentation of a brochure of twenty-eight floor plans, Smith, Jones, and Contini purchased a lot in Mount Washington, a community northeast of downtown Los Angeles. With confidence in their designs and also a vested interest on the part of Contini and Jones, who had purchased memberships in the MHA, the architects set out to prove the viability and beauty of their creations. Out of their own funds, they paid for the construction of the MHA model 109 to serve as a pilot house. As the more Wrightian of the designs and the design with the most dramatic mix of exposed materials and inventive details, the Pilot House springs from a concrete masonry abutment to cantilever on two steel beams over the hillside. The wood structure above consisted of wood framing that FHA had not allowed yet. The roof was made of two-inch tongue-and-groove

Pilot House under construction, Mt. Washington, 1947
Opposite: 1947 Brochure for Mutual Housing Association featuring the Pilot House in Mt. Washington

planks with seven-foot on-center beams, typical of all the proposed MHA designs.

Due to its location and cost overruns, the architects lost money on their experiment, but the Pilot House (MHA model 109) was considered a huge benefit to the MHA members. Since few members had firsthand knowledge of architecture or knew how to read plans, the Pilot House allowed them to experience the architecture in person, revel in the experimental form, and understand the concept of exposed structure and materials. The Pilot House delighted the MHA membership; it should, however, have given them a hint of the financial problems to come. The construction cost far exceeded what the architectural team had hoped to spend on this experiment; as a result only a handful of model 109 and the similar 108 homes were built within

the community.

After the completion of the Pilot House in Mount Washington, the team had another opportunity to improve on the construction methods for hillside houses. With the financial support of the membership, the first structure built in the Crestwood Hills community resembled the Pilot House but without any interior walls. Situated next to the area designated for the cooperative facilities and the park, this structure served as the site office where the architects worked and where members could meet and choose their house plans.The structure was intended to become the arts-and-crafts building once the community was completed.

Top: Pilot House living room · *Bottom:* Pilot House bedroom
Opposite: Pilot House kitchen and bedroom from brochure

kitchen

Separated from the dining area by a serving counter,
is the kichen. Below view windows is a
stainless steel sink, with garbage disposal unit,
and plastic topped counters.
Close by are the range burners with exhaust fans above,
and a separate, work height oven unit.
Ample storage is provided. The walls are washable,
and the cork floor resilient.

8

bedroom no. 1

Space is adequate for
either double or twin beds.
Parapet storage, a small
makeup table, and a
generous wardrobe are built-
in. All wardrobe doors
may be opened at once, and
their backs provide
additional useful space.
Indirect light above
the wardrobe lights both
room and wardrobe.

9

CHAPTER THREE

Development

After interviewing more than six hundred applicants, MHA reached its full membership of five hundred by the beginning of 1948. The group included professors from UCLA, mathematicians, psychiatrists, musicians, lawyers, and accountants. More than fifty professions were represented in the membership lists. The number of obstetricians and psychiatrists among the members inspired the remark that Crestwood Hills is the ideal place to start a family or have a nervous breakdown.

Jules Salkin, as the executive director, had a great deal of the cooperative's cash at his disposal and shopped around town for the equipment needed to develop the property; he often purchased large pieces of army-surplus machinery. Soon after the first year, auditors found mysterious undocumented debits in the accounts. When Salkin was questioned, he offered a story about buying bulldozers, but actually he had used the money to make a personal loan. Several on the board, shocked by the news about the loan, felt he was taking too much control; some called him was a crook. Asked to leave the cooperative that he had initiated,

Salkin was distraught but agreed to resign; he did so one month after the architects were hired. Ray Siegel recalled, "It was a crushing blow to Jules; it was his baby." George Brown, Jr., replaced Salkin as executive director.

The groundbreaking ceremony took place at 2 p.m. on October 5, 1947. More than three hundred MHA members and their guests gathered to hear Robert Alexander, an architect and vice president of the Los Angeles City Planning Commission, speak about the importance of bringing good architecture to the people through the cooperative movement as a practical solution to the high cost of housing. By that time, the Board had confirmed that four hundred lots were to be developed. The chairman of the board, William M. Brown, introduced the board of directors and the general manager, Everett R. Harman. Harman related briefly the history of the development and its progress to date. Edgardo Contini, on behalf of the architects, described the status of the house plans, some of which were to be shown to the members and their friends the following month. As the ceremony drew to a

Opposite: Mutual Housing Association groundbreaking, October 1947

Groundbreaking with a plant nursery in the background

close, a bulldozer belonging to J.A. Thompson, the contractor handling the early grading, appeared on the hilltop, cutting a new road in its path: a dramatic new beginning.

The following year, in 1948, Seaboard Engineering began laying out the roads. MHA's first paid manager, Robert Graves, had the difficult task of satisfying a thousand bosses (five hundred couples). He suggested designing the community for four hundred houses, but the board of directors decreed five hundred houses were necessary to make the project feasible; the board set the program at five hundred lots for homes and additional land for various public amenities, only to revert to the four hundred-house total a few months later when membership declined and each tract contained fewer buildable lots than proposed.

Contrary to the prevailing tradition of building homes on flat land in canyon floors to make construction relatively easy and inexpensive, the MHA opted for the desirable light and views that building on hillsides afforded, and left the canyon flats for public amenities. As a result of this unrealistic vision, the land development alone cost a

Top: Edgardo Contini leading MHA members on a site selection day. · Bottom: Members on site selection day on Hanley Avenue

Grading for MHA development, 1947

million dollars and required moving 2.5 million cubic yards of earth on 370 acres (In Los Angeles, moving that much earth for a single project was only exceeded when the 405 freeway was cut through the Sepulveda pass in the late 1950s.) The design team used a stepped terrace plan for grading the hillside, which would afford most houses views of the Santa Monica Bay and city lights below. The lots are relatively small, but the topography and the positioning of the houses at odd angles provide a great deal of privacy between each house. Each house has two or three important faces, one to the street, which emphasized the sense of community, one to a private open space, and one, which could

be the same as the second, to the view. In this way, each house achieves the goal of both being private and being part of a community.

Although potential members initially had been told the properties would average $2,000, a real estate professional determined the *actual* cost of each lot. The costs of developing various properties added to the final price of the lots, which ranged from $1,900 to $5,000, depending on size, location, and views. Maps were posted and members chose their lots depending on their priority number, a number that represented when they joined MHA.

Initially, MHA did not have sufficient membership to develop the entire eight hundred acres,

so it started by creating one tract at a time. As each of the four tracts was developed, the Architecture Committee drew up that tract's covenants, conditions, and restrictions (CC&Rs).

All new CC&Rs included a clause requiring an Architecture Committee to oversee design to keep the community consistent with the progressive modernist architecture—and the guidelines aimed to ensure consistent scale and landscape conditions. The MHA joint venture of Jones, Smith, and Contini had participated in founding the Crestwood Hills Architecture Committee and creating the original Architectural Guidelines. Jones and Smith designed the committee to

be self-selecting, intending to keep tight control on the designs of remodels and new construction. The committee still consists of two architects and a third member, a layman in the community.

Each of the four separate tracts in Crestwood Hills maintains the same philosophy in its guidelines: the need for the houses to blend into the hillside rather than making individual architectural statements. Houses were required to all be one story to prevent canyonization, a perceived narrowing of the streets by tall buildings on each side. The architectural objective is stated clearly in the guidelines:

1. To promote thoughtful design so that there is harmony between buildings

Aerial view of the Mutual Housing Site Office after completion in 1948

and their sites and with neighboring homes, avoiding harsh contrasts in the visual perception of the community,

2. To encourage the maintenance of building forms which readily become part of the terrain rather than intruding into it and commanding attention, and

3. To strive for designs, selected materials, colors and finishes, and total site planning that seek these objectives.

The guidelines were specific on nearly every aspect of construction, including materials, colors, and window placement; even exterior lighting was addressed: "All exterior lighting shall be designed and installed that the light source of any exterior lighting fixture shall not be visible from neighboring properties."

The Board created a Tree Committee to enforce the guideline rule that all hedges and trees were to be no higher than six feet. Violations to this requirement abound, given the nature of plant material and most homeowners' unsophisticated plant selections. Landscape designs that don't follow an overall plan have resulted in continual complaints from owners of obstructed views. Primary views are protected by CC&Rs, and the Tree Committee's rulings about obstructions have prevailed consistently in court cases.

The first tract, at the lower part of the property, was flatter than the upper slopes. After witnessing the complexity and cost of the Pilot House in Mount Washington, the majority of the members preferred to build on a flat lot. There were, however, only seventy-five flat lots proposed. The MHA model 111X, a much simpler design than the Pilot House, with its simple low, sloping gable roof and limited use of masonry block, an element that contributed to its cost-effectiveness, was most suitable for the flatter lots. Ray Siegel, one of the founding members selected the 111, as did nearly all of the homeowners on Deerbrook Lane. MHA model 702X was the second most popular model selected, also ideal for a flat lot.

In 1948, the association distributed to the membership a sales brochure with a photograph on the cover of the site office. Houses were designed to appeal to moderate-income families, and at the time, that meant families whose breadwinner made about $10,000. Each of the twenty-eight house plans was represented on a two-page spread containing a description, floor plan, elevations, the proposed square footage of the house and carport, and a perspective drawing of either the interior or the exterior of the house. The smallest house plan was 775 square feet and was estimated to cost $8,500 to $9,100. The largest house built was 1850 square feet for an approximate cost of $19,560.

Grouping of MHA houses on Rochedale Lane, part of the first thirty houses built in 1948

House Construction

As house plans were selected and owners attempted to secure FHA-insured mortgage loans, the FHA threw up another seemingly unsurmountable barrier; they would not loan to "modern" house design, rejecting post and beam and hillside construction. A committee of MHA members flew to Washington D.C. to confront the FHA and argue their case. The mission was successful with FHA making an exemption, approving loans for the structures as "experimental."

With funds in place, the contractor planned to build the first thirty houses, followed by groups of fifteen houses started two weeks later and then fifteen houses two weeks after that until all the lots had been built upon. The first thirty members to build their MHA houses were considered the guinea pigs; no one knew what would be the final cost of building the houses, whether they would actually serve their families well, or be completed on time to meet the deadlines set by their FHA loans. The handsome palette of finishing materials cost far more than originally estimated, as did the electric kitchens with the newest Thermador appliances. As it turned out, the first thirty families were the luckiest; their houses were built with quality and

integrity. Because the houses were so complicated to build, the contractor, Womack Company, had underestimated the construction expense, and was forced into bankruptcy in 1950, after absorbing about three thousand dollars in cost overruns for each house.

For the second group of thirty houses to be built further up Deerbrook Lane, Tigertail Road, and Lindenwood, the association picked a contractor from San Diego. The contractor completed only fifteen of the houses before he, too, left the project due to cost overruns, in the midst of construction. This resulted in liens from sub-contractors who had not been paid. Builders for Joint Control, a bonding company that had insured the second group, took over finishing most of the houses but not all. Members were then left to complete the work themselves or make deals with the subcontractors who had already worked on the project. There was additional pressure in meeting deadlines set by the financing institutions.

With all the challenges of developing the lots on difficult topography and the resultant rise in the lot cost, MHA members started to worry that they would not have a house by the time they needed it. Their limited funds were being used up; some dropped out due to cost overruns. After a time, there were more members wishing to drop out than those wishing to join.

Expressing his frustration with the runaway costs of the development, actor Fritz Feld abandoned hopes of building an MHA-designed home and wrote an angry letter to MHA General Manager Robert Graves, accusing the architects of defying the interests of the small income members in preference to the more financially secure. He cited the architects' delay in submitting acceptable plans in time for the site selection day, which caused many members to choose plans without sufficient time to study the plans and understand what they had selected. Feld also complained that the cost of lots had gone up—without any assessment or vote—from $2,000 to $5,000. He had asked about the rising costs of the architectural designs at every meeting, warning members that costs were increasing and that many would not have the money for upkeep, furniture, landscaping, or even basics like food and medical needs.

An article in the *Hollywood Citizen-News* in June 1950 estimated that MHA houses would cost $15,000 for the complete package including lot, house, landscaping, and one of the five hundred shares of MHA itself, which would fund the communal facilities. By comparison, the Eichler

Homes in Northern California originally sold for $9,500 all-inclusive. The newly established $15,000 price tag was a stretch for a moderate-income family; several families became discouraged and found cheaper solutions.

Those who withdrew formed a group known as the Withdrawees. Together, they hoped to recoup the money they had invested. Unfortunately for them, the MHA bylaws set the condition that money could not be returned to an investor unless he or she found someone to take their place in the membership. The Association had first priority in the repurchase of the land, but soon MHA was not

Eichler Home

in a financial position to repurchase their shares. According to Gerald Tannen, at the time the second tract was developed, the Withdrawees had no choice but to sue MHA for their money. Although the Withdrawees prevailed in court, they received only the book value of their original shares.

The MHA financial position became untenable, so the organization disbanded. With its dissolution, there was no mechanism for managing the finances of the development. Lots could not be bought and sold through the MHA; Crestwood Hills suddenly became just another homeowners association.

But the MHA had been successful in creating a community, and at least a few of the founders' cooperative ideas not only materialized, but outlived the original association. The credit union lasted until the late 1980s. The association had funded a small structure, just below the site office, an MHA model 104, which served as the contractor's office during construction. After the second contractor left the project, the contractor's building was converted to a nursery school. Community members established the Crestwood Hills Cooperative Nursery School with thirty or forty students and the participation of parents to maintain the

Crestwood Hills Nursery School

1

2

3

4

Builders' Homes for Better Living

A. Quincy Jones
Frederick E. Emmons
John L. Chapman
Associate

Reinhold

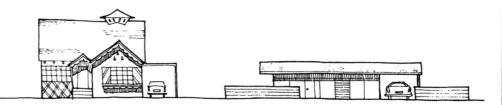

The two houses above are drawn exactly the same width, and illustrate the application of this principle. By extending the roof overhangs, providing unbroken ridge and eave lines, and by adding horizontal fences, the right hand house not only appears larger, but tends to flow together as a harmonious design rather than a collection of unrelated units.

The sketches below show two other ways in which the appearance of houses may be improved.

The combination of window and door openings, with the alignment of their heads and sills, along with the widely projecting eaves, provides a better proportion and helps to eliminate the "boxy" look.

In the book *Builders' Homes for Better Living* (1957) by A. Quincy Jones and Frederick E. Emmons, the authors occasionally use examples of MHA houses to explain their points, and discuss the importance of considered site planning for hillside homes. The publication explains the logical approach to good builders' house design in simple terms with many illustrations. MHA architect Jones felt builders' house designs should not just provide shelter but create a way of living, a concept he saw through to completion in the MHA community. The lower illustrations are of MHA houses on Stonehill Lane.

The simplification of the roof by reducing projections and planes to a long, unbroken pitch gives an appearance of added width.

structure and grounds and serve as teachers' assistants. As of this writing, the school still exists, with more than seventy students, the largest cooperative nursery school in Southern California. Residents of Crestwood Hills are given preference in enrollment for the nursery school and other families compete to enlist their children. Set among the sycamores and pine trees near Crestwood Hills Park, the school begun by Elizabeth Israel and Kit Anderson continues to encourage children to learn through play.

MHA had served as the agency brokering the sale of individual lots to members, but once the corporation was dissolved, members who wanted sell or buy a lot in Crestwood Hills were in trouble: no real estate company would broker a transaction. Indeed, many local real estate brokers felt nothing but disdain for a cooperative community that was not particularly affluent. So, in an effort to meet this need, residents Myer Bello and Leonard Krupnick set up a small real estate office in a room in the nursery school building. Both men were musicians working in the same movie production studio and had flexible schedules. They became licensed brokers, carrying on the hands-on approach that had created the community.

Hermann and Vida Schott purchased a lot on Bluegrass Lane but grew impatient waiting for builders to construct the house they selected,

Crestwood Hills Nursery School in foreground,
MHA Site Office in background

so they purchased the fourth house built in the community that served as the model home. It had opened to the public in May of 1950, furnished per the architect's specifications. Julius Shulman extensively photographed the house that year.

Strongly supporting the idea of a cooperative community, Schott was referred to by another early MHA member, Saul Braverman, as "one of the great white knights; lending money to the association, bailing them out of several binds, and building Crestwood Stables."

Prior to the MHA development, horse stables and a saloon operated just outside Crestwood Hills behind the Sturges House on Skyewiay Road. Designed by Frank Lloyd Wright, this dignified structure gave no clue as to the activities at the nearby establishment. The Alturus Inn was not just a bar; it was complete with dance floor, jukebox, and rooms rented by the hour, a Depression-era respite for where both locals and transplants working in the burgeoning wartime aviation industry could kick up their heels. Ben Weber rented the stables, and Eric Schott, Hermann's son, worked for Weber part time.

In 1952, Hermann Schott purchased seventy-five acres west of the area the MHA had developed as a park, hiring Weber to construct horse stables and a small tack house for the Crestwood Hills community. Evening hayrides and dances were held at the stables, and on October 18, 1953, the first annual horse show, sponsored by the Crestwood Saddle Club, was held there.

Schott also created the Cottonwood Canyon Company to build facilities for a swim school and day camp, with hopes of also building an

Schott House, Mutual Housing model 702, fourth house built in the community and used as a model house

Top: Schott House kitchen · *Bottom:* Schott House living room, furniture selected by the MHA joint venture, photographed by Julius Shulman. Note the vertical louvers on the exterior, facing west. · *Opposite:* Schott House MHA 702

next to the clubhouse. The entire south side of the clubhouse opened up to the amphitheater providing a large area for a stage. The amphitheater was rarely used until the show business veteran, Fritz Feld, and his actress wife Virginia Christine (renowned as the Folger's Coffee lady, "Mrs. Olsen"), lured musicians, dancers, actors, speakers, and other artists to perform for the community. Although the Felds, members since December 1947, decided against building an MHA house, they built one of the fine modernist houses on Rochedale Lane in 1957. They were deeply committed to the community of Crestwood Hills and Brentwood in general, both serving as honorary mayors of Brentwood in 1979. The amphitheater was renamed the Fritz Feld Community Theatre in 1978. As late as the early 2000s, the occasional performance took

Fritz Feld and his wife, Virginia Christine.

place at the theater.

Despite financial difficulties, the community became a landmark of modern housing design. An

The early scheme for the park clubhouse and cooperative facilities · *Opposite*: Detail of beam to post, MHA 702

Top: Mutual Housing model 111X, the most popular model in the community · *Bottom*: MX108X

Top: MHA model 111 · Bottom: Freiler House, MHA 702 in foreground, Schott House in background, Schneidman House on the hill behind

Rochedale Lane houses

MUTUAL HOUSING ASSOCIATION
A PROJECT FOR FIVE HUNDRED FAMILIES IN CRESTWOOD HILLS
WHITNEY R. SMITH, A. QUINCY JONES, EDGARDO CONTINI
ARCHITECTS, ENGINEERS AND SITE PLANNERS
JAMES CHARLTON, WAYNE R. WILLIAMS, COLLABORATING

Arts and Architecture article on Mutual Housing,
September 1948

extensive fourteen-page article ran in *Arts and Architecture* magazine in September 1948, showcasing the plans for the community and the various floor plans and elevations of the houses. In 1952, the AIA gave the Award of Merit to the original five-hundred-house plan. The remaining original MHA houses have stood the test of time—they were not just architecturally innovative, they were also structurally sound. Only one house suffered a cracked pane of glass in the Northridge earthquake of 1994, a testament to the quality of the design and careful construction.

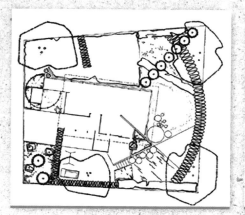
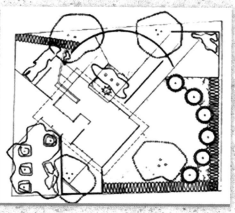
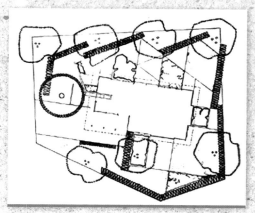

Top: MHA individual house plans, Garrett Eckbo   *Bottom:* Perspective of Crestwood Hills by Garrett Eckbo

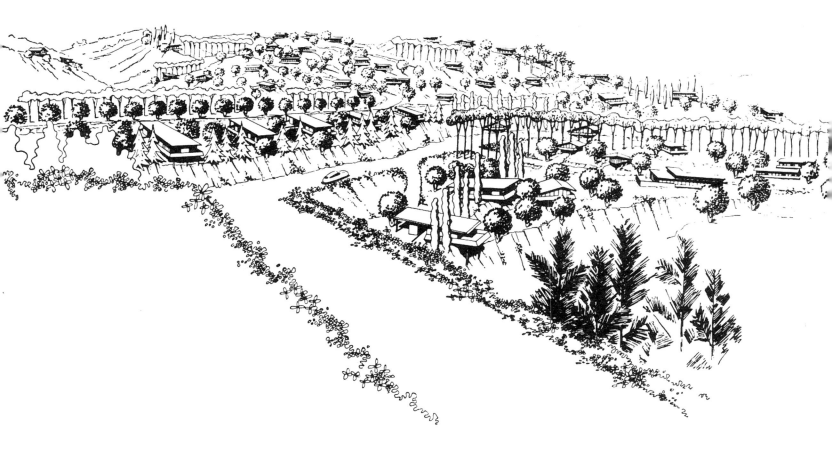

Friedman House MHA 403 showing bedroom partition open

Infill Houses

Each progressive stage of tract development featured fewer and fewer MHA-designed houses. The first developed tract, (14944, recorded in mid-1949) had just over seventy MHA-designed houses. The next year the second tract, (14122, referred to as the East Ridge) included only a few original designs along the eastern side of Tigertail Road. There were none of the original MHA designs in the third tract (15905, known as the West Ridge), which ran along Kenter Avenue. A fourth tract, 16210, at the top of Tigertail, was developed in 1951 as the second portion of the East Ridge.

Of the 350 established lots in Crestwood Hills, about three-quarters housed structures that were outside the original MHA design plan. Because of the rising costs of developing the land and expense of constructing the MHA houses, many members chose to hire their own architects and builders. Other disgruntled members, known as "the Withdrawees," sold their undeveloped lots to escape the increased financial burden of building on the land, and new property owners chose their own creative teams. Despite being the majority of homes in Crestwood Hills, these projects became known as "infill" houses, a term often used in urban planning to describe areas filled in between existing structures.

Dwindling membership and repayments to Withdrawees weakened the financial stability of the MHA. To obtain the money owed to the Withdrawees, land surrounding the tracts was sold off. The remainder of the tract that contained property that extended down to Bundy Drive was sold to a developer. Most of the property on the west side of northern Kenter was taken over by a developer, Grandview Construction, and became an area now known as Brentwood Estates, which basically conformed to the architectural intent of the MHA community.

Many of those who purchased the undeveloped lots were of a higher economic bracket than the original MHA members. The new group included doctors, psychiatrists, business owners, and other professionals. They had the financial resources to hire outstanding architects practicing in Los Angeles at that time. Among the infill houses were many designed by well-known architects who became synonymous with the city's mid-century architecture: Craig Ellwood, Richard Neutra, Rodney Walker, Ray Kappe, Thornton Abell, Welton S. Beckett, J.R. Davidson, and Cliff May. Lesser known but accomplished architects such as Carlton

Winslow were also represented in the community. One of the four founding members, Jules Salkin, later became an architect and designed a house for the Gordon family on Deerbrook Lane. Alfred T. Wilkes, who was also a member of the community, Kazumi Adachi, and the team of Palmer, Krisel, Lindsey designed more than one house in the community, as did Beckett and Walker.

Some members chose to commission custom designs by the original MHA architects. Gerald Tannen and his first wife, who suffered from polio, originally hoped to build an MHA model 403 on two lots at the top of Tigertail on Chickory Lane. Instead they hired A. Quincy Jones to build a custom house on the site that accommodated her special needs.

The community experienced an aesthetic shift after the Bel Air fire of 1961, which destroyed forty-nine of the houses in Crestwood Hills. Very few of the owners of destroyed MHA houses chose to rebuild from the original designs. The Tannen House designed by Jones was rebuilt per original plans. MHA member Gerald Tannen had a large darkroom with flat files in which he stored the original MHA plans. His house—and the plans—and A. Quincy Jones's own house down a long driveway off Tigertail burned to the ground.

Building requirements changed after the fire with an emphasis on fire-resistant construction.

Seismic requirements had been upgraded, which increased the construction cost to rebuild an original MHA house. Among the few who stayed with the original aesthetic, Ray Kappe designed another "burn-out" on Lindenwood, taking great care to reflect the character of the surviving MHA originals, with a dramatic sloping roof and clerestory windows. Other houses of note have been demolished or remodeled beyond recognition, including the J.R. Davidson Farber House on Rochedale Lane, the Cliff May Colver House on Tigertail Road, and the Keyser House on Stonehill Lane designed by Rodney Walker.

With renewed interest in the original MHA houses, new owners are taking care to preserve the unique character of the buildings and to respect the design team's original intentions. Three Craig Ellwood houses, Ray Kappe's three houses, Rodney Walker's Knauer House, and Neutra's Adler House have all stood the test of time. Ellwood's Johnson House has been restored faithfully to its original condition, as has Kappe's Gould-LaFetra House.

Many of the remaining MHA houses have been declared City of Los Angeles Historic-Cultural Monuments, and several streets in Crestwood Hills retain their original character, a delight for all those who wish to explore this fascinating experiment that combined cooperative living and modern architecture.

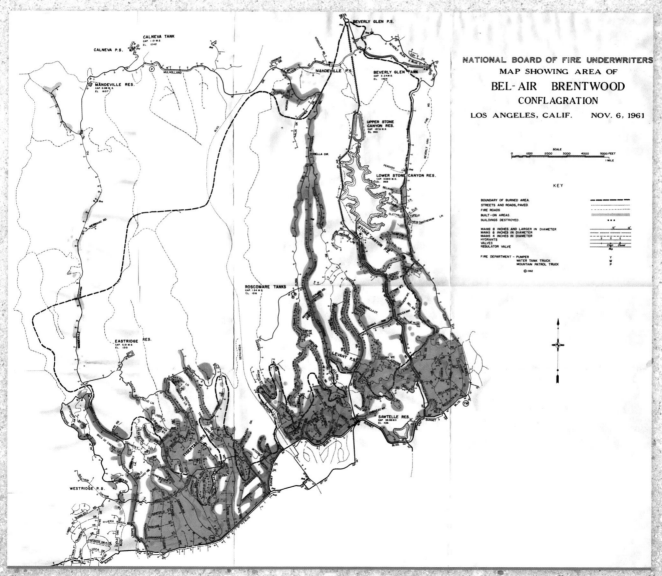

NATIONAL BOARD OF FIRE UNDERWRITERS
MAP SHOWING AREA OF
BEL-AIR BRENTWOOD
CONFLAGRATION
LOS ANGELES, CALIF.   NOV. 6, 1961

The 1961 Bel Air Fire destroyed one-fourth of the buildings in its path.
Of the 505 structures destroyed, forty-nine were homes in Crestwood Hills

Crestwood Hills Today

With very few of the cooperative facilities realized, the community of Crestwood Hills proved less a cooperative community than an architectural statement with a few shared amenities. The original concept of providing a credit union, medical office, grocery store, community center with a restaurant, plant nursery, beauty parlor, nursery school, and gas station proved overly ambitious. By the time the houses were completed, the only facilities established were the nursery school, the credit union, and plans for a park with a community center.

The credit union survived for many years, paying interest to the investors, under the direction of Hermann Schott and Helen Keyser. A young Harold Meyerson took out a car loan through the credit union, which proved to be at a much lower rate than the local banks could offer. He presented an application to the Credit Union Committee and received approval. Peter Israel, the son of the original members Marion and Elizabeth, had become a depositor at the age of eight, and used the credit union well into adulthood for car loans, law school financing, and a mortgage. By 1989, the credit union had assets close to a half-million dollars and only two thousand dollars in defaulted loans. Nevertheless,

it closed in the early 1990s due to lack of activity.

Despite the failure to create a true cooperative, a collective consciousness that goes beyond socializing with neighbors has always been a part of Crestwood Hills. Hundreds of dedicated people have served tirelessly on the Crestwood Hills Association board and committees, publishing the newsletter and organizing community events in an effort to keep the community residents connected. The park still draws families for Monday pizza night and weekly "Mommy and Me" classes. An annual softball game always draws crowds to play on the baseball diamond laid out and built by volunteers more than sixty years ago, and the annual Crestwood Hills Association meeting brings out the largest number of members. Dinner is served and often lectures are presented before the election of board members and an open public discussion.

As original Crestwood Hills members age and leave the community, the history and stories of the founding of Crestwood Hills start to fade, but the tradition of getting together or helping a neighbor still continues, and the preserved MHA houses serve as a constant reminder of the dynamic history of this unique community.

Opposite: Alex and Kristin MacDowell in their Schneidman House

Situated west of the San Diego Freeway, the Getty Center, and Mt. St. Mary's College, Crestwood Hills is north of (and accessed via) Sunset Boulevard. Mapped here are the forty-seven remaining houses of MHA design, along with significant infill houses.

1. MHA Site Office; MHA 102, 990 Hanley Avenue (HCM #680)
2. Dolman House; MHA 103, 967 Bluegrass Lane
3. Arens House; MHA 104, 12436 Deerbrook Lane (HCM #720)
4. Brown House; MHA 104, 12376 Deerbrook Lane
5. Crestwood Hills Nursery School; MHA 104, 986 Hanley Avenue
6. Hart House; MHA 104, 12444 Rochedale Lane
7. Gelb House; MHA 104X, 12450 Rochedale Lane
8. Sonin House; MHA 104X, 1046 N. Tigertail Road
9. Israel House; MHA 105, 914 Bluegrass Lane (HCM #693)
10. Scott House; MHA 106, 955 Stonehill Lane
11. Sherwood House; MHA 108, 947 Stonehill Lane (HCM #698)
12. Brach House; MHA 108X, 918 N. Tigertail Road
13. Henstell House; MHA 108X, 815 N. Tigertail Road
14. Tritel House; MHA 110, 716 Rochedale Way
15. Gross House; MHA 111, 860 Hanley Avenue (HCM #695)
16. Hamma House; MHA 111, 12404 Deerbrook Lane (HCM #797)
17. Siegel House; MHA 111, 12400 Deerbrook Lane
18. Gorgan House; MHA 111X, 12449 Deerbrook Lane
19. Haas House; MHA 111X, 12404 Rochedale Lane (HCM #633)
20. Kalmick House; MHA 111X, 12327 Rochedale Lane (HCM #634)
21. Kalmick House; MHA 111X, 12408 Rochedale Lane
22. Palmer House; MHA 111X, 800 Hanley Avenue
23. Royer House; MHA 111X, 12421 Deerbrook Lane
24. Schou House; MHA 111X, 12420 Deerbrook Lane
25. Stoleroff House; MHA 111X, 12367 Deerbrook Lane (HCM #721)
26. Volk House; MHA 111X, 12412 Deerbrook Lane (HCM #722)
27. Wurtele House; MHA 111X, 946 Stonehill Lane (HCM #723)
28. Schneidman House; MHA 301, 925 Stonehill Lane (HCM #1016)

29. Kermin House; MHA 302, 900 Stonehill Lane (HCM #697)
30. Brite House; MHA 401, 872 Hanley Avenue
31. Heilpern House; MHA 401, 12421 Rochedale Lane
32. Miller House; MHA 401X, 12420 Rochedale Lane (HCM #862)
33. Sidney Silver House; MHA 401X, 901 Bluegrass Lane
34. Becker House; MHA 402, 12438 Rochedale Lane
35. Wasserberger House; MHA 402, 12415 Rochedale Lane
36. Friedman House; MHA 403, 12414 Rochedale Lane
37. Alexander House; MHA 702, 12400 Rochedale Lane
38. Anderson House; MHA 702, 12427 Rochedale Lane
39. Eiduson House; MHA 702, 941 Stonehill Lane
40. Freiler House; MHA 702, 861 Hanley Avenue
41. Goldenfeld House; MHA 702, 810 Bramble Way (HCM #632)
42. Grant House; MHA 702, 815 Bramble Way
43. Pezman House; MHA 702, 12320 Deerbrook Lane
44. Rice House; MHA 702, 12354 Rochedale Lane
45. Schott House; MHA 702, 907 Hanley Avenue (HCM #682)
46. Stein House; MHA 702, 968 Stonehill Lane (HCM #1015)
47. Weckler House; MHA 702, 12434 Rochedale Lane (HCM #635)
48. Jones House; A. Quincy Jones (1953), 1233 N. Tigertail Road
49. Tannen House; A. Quincy Jones (1953, rebuilt 1962), 1230 Chickory Lane
50. Zack House; Craig Ellwood (1952), 1036 N. Tigertail Road
51. Johnson House; Craig Ellwood (1952), 1515 N. Tigertail Road
52. Levey House; Craig Ellwood (1958), 1095 N. Kenter Avenue
53. Knauer House; Rodney Walker (1954), 921 Bluegrass Lane
54. Keyser House; Rodney Walker (1952), 942 Stonehill Lane
55. Gould/LaFetra House; Ray Kappe (1967), 12256 Canna Road (HCM #886)
56. Gale House; Ray Kappe (1962), 1009 Lindenwood Lane
57. Brody House; Ray Kappe (1960), 936 Kenter Way
58. Adler House; Richard Neutra (1956), 1438 N. Kenter Avenue
59. Sale House; Richard Neutra (1960), 1531 N. Tigertail Road

PART TWO

Individual House Descriptions

Mutual Housing Association Tract Houses

The sheer inventiveness of the twenty-eight house plans represented in the booklet *Mutual Plans*, and the enthusiasm that the membership felt towards the architect's presentation is evident in the MHA models selected for the first tract 14944. Most of tract 14944 was fairly flat and suitable for the designs for flat lots or those that could accommodate slightly sloping lots. Out of 126 selections, twenty were for MHA 111X, nine for MHA 111 and nine for MHA 702. The remainder of the house designs, noted in an early list of members and the house designs they chose, varied widely but did not include the very large and costly hillside models. Models of all sizes contained elements of sophisticated design and consideration. Even the smallest model, MHA 110 at 775 square feet, featured a long exposed concrete block wall that supports the structure on one end and continues to enclose a terrace on the other with a dramatic pitched shed roof.

Opposite: Schneidman House, MHA 301 · *Overleaf:* MHA Site Office

MHA Site Office, MHA 101 modified
(2 bedrooms, 2 bathrooms, 1035 square feet, $12,742)

Shortly after the completion of the Mount Washington Pilot House, a similar structure was built on the Brentwood land, near the proposed communal area. Upon completion, the original office on Robertson Boulevard moved to this MHA Site Office, which also served as an office for the architects and a display area where members could review plans and select their lots and house models.

Similar to the MHA model 101, but built without interior walls, the Site Office featured a long concrete masonry wall that ran the entire length of the one-story portion of the house and extended into the garden, creating a dynamic horizontality. In addition, a five-foot-high garden wall was placed perpendicular to the structural wall and carried through the house where it incorporated a distinctive cantilevered fireplace.

Consistent in the design of all MHA models, the structure featured exposed post and beams at seven-foot spacing, exposed tongue-and-groove ceiling, exposed redwood siding, and exposed concrete masonry block. The dramatically angled building section, with its brise-soleil and clerestory windows, is reminiscent of Wright's Taliesin West and Broadacre City hillside houses; these echoes of Wright are due to Taliesin apprentices Jim Charlton and Wayne Williams, who worked in the joint-venture office.

The house is built on an uphill slope, providing an area underneath the house for two parking spaces and the start of the entry steps. The main floor spans across the carport supported on two steel I-beams which are supported on a wide concrete block pilaster.

In 1951, William Kerman and his wife, Gussie, purchased the MHA Site Office from the community and converted it to a house using the MHA 101 as a guide. Kerman, a businessman, was very familiar with the Site Office, where he had served on the MHA Commercial Facilities Committee, Interviewing Committee, and Architectural Committee. His three brothers, Bernard, Gene, and Henry, also bought into MHA.

MHA Site Office // Restoration: Nick Roberts, AIA, and Cory Buckner, Architect

Opposite top: Daylight view of former MHA Site Office · *Opposite bottom*: Nighttime view

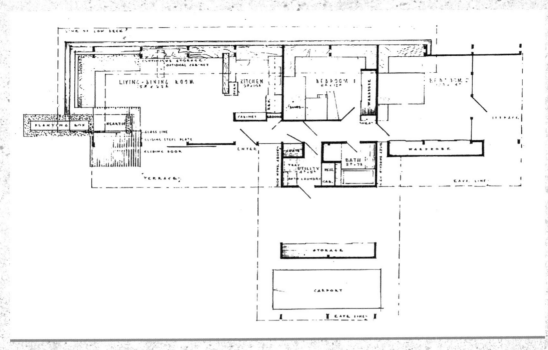

Top: MHA 101 floor plan · *Bottom*: Dining room · *Opposite*: MHA Site Office kitchen

Arens House rear elevation

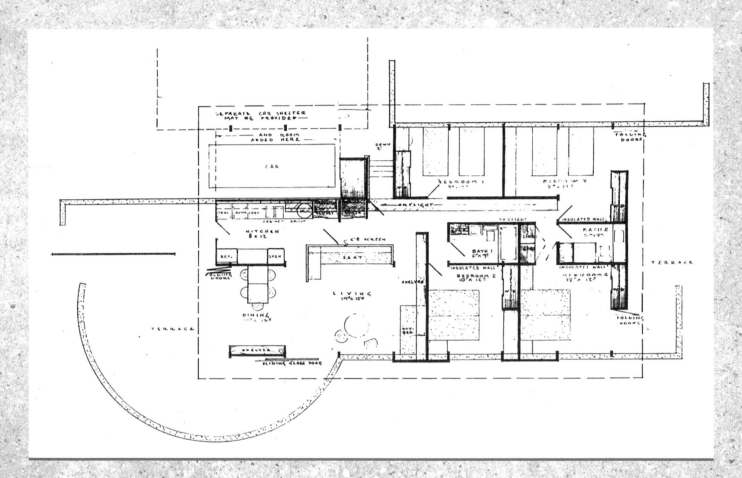

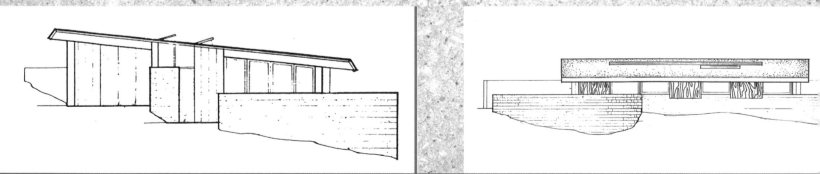

MHA 104X plan and elevation

MHA 104X
(4 bedrooms, 2 bathrooms, 1370 square feet, $14,493)

Similar to the MHA 104, the MHA model 104X featured a masonry fireplace as the central focus of the house. Added to the basic 104 floorplan were two additional bedrooms and an additional bathroom.

Planned to be built on a mild downhill slope, the house is sheltered under a gently angled roof that extends toward the private driveway, creating a carport space. Skylights along the center ridge beam shed sunlight into the kitchen and entry area.

Morris and Lydia Gelb were the original owners of an MHA 104X house on Rochedale Lane, where they raised their two daughters.

Gelb House // Restoration by owners Landis Green and Bruce Norelius, architect

Gelb House rear elevation

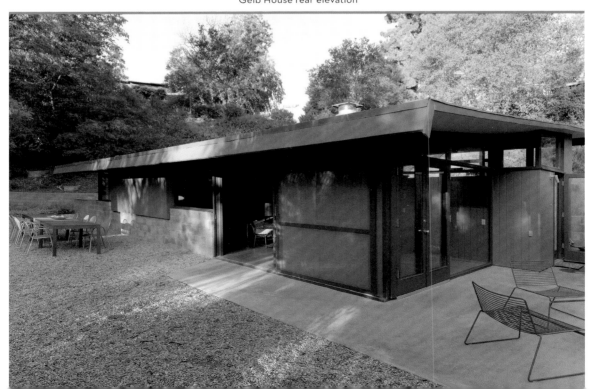

Top: Gelb House view from dining area towards kitchen
Bottom left: Gelb House living room view towards garden · Bottom right: Gelb House living room · Opposite: Gelb House hallway

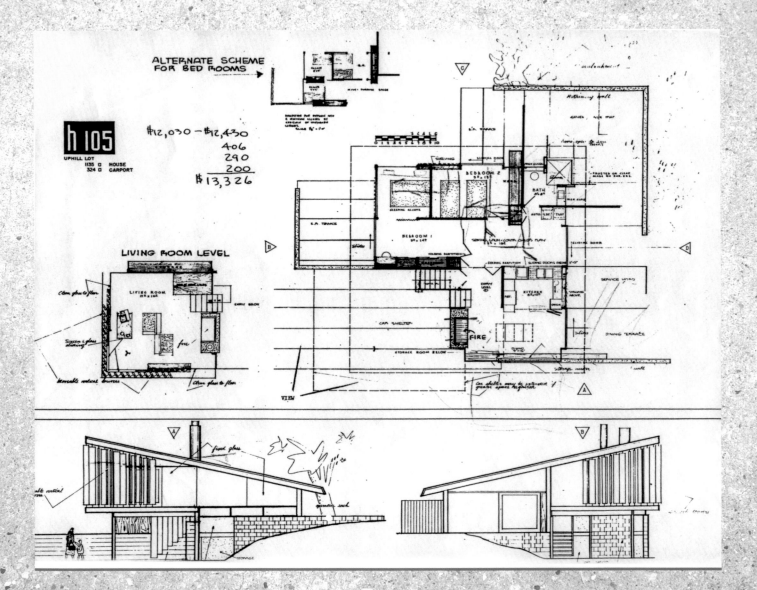

MHA 105 floor plan and elevations

MHA 105
(2 bedrooms, 1 bathroom, 1135 square feet, $13,326)

Only ten sites were originally designated for the MHA model 105 and only two MHA 105 homes were actually built; the Israel House and the Hermann House at 12317 Rochedale Lane, which still stands but has been remodeled beyond recognition.

Built for approximately $13,300 and considered a hillside model, the MHA 105 features a living room with corner sliding glass doors and exterior vertical louvers made of redwood. The movable louvers (now removed from the Israel House) were used to control the solar gain within the house since the living room is facing southwest, the direction of the Santa Monica Bay view. The split-level fireplace opens at floor level at the living room and at waist level at the dining room. The kitchen opens to the dining room with a view to the fireplace. Unlike most houses in the neighborhood, the original plywood on the Israel house has never been painted; it has aged to a golden brown which complements the aged pink concrete masonry walls throughout the house.

The Israel family originally owned the one extant MHA 105. Active in the community from an early date, Jerry Israel was a professional preschool teacher and started the Crestwood Hills Nursery School with another teacher, Kit Anderson. Marion Israel served as president of the Crestwood Hills Board and served on the Architecture Committee many years.

Israel House dining room

Top: Sherwood House rear elevation · Bottom: master bedroom
Opposite: Sherwood House living room showing movable clerestory panel in open position

MHA 111
(2 bedrooms, 2 bathrooms, 1060 square feet, $10,966)

One of the smallest models in the community, MHA model 111 is distinguished from model 111X by its smaller footprint of 1060 square feet and by the lack of a fireplace. The living room, dining area, and kitchen are on one level, unlike model 111X, and instead of the dynamic fireplace, a tongue-and-groove redwood wall extends from the exterior of the house into the interior living area. Simple finishes include plywood kitchen cabinets left exposed with just a light stain revealing the wood grain. The pink concrete masonry units are left exposed throughout.

Gross House // Restoration: Cory Buckner, Architect

Gross House rear elevation · Opposite: Gross House study

Top: Gross House living room. · *Bottom*: MHA 111 floor plan · *Opposite*: Gross House entrance

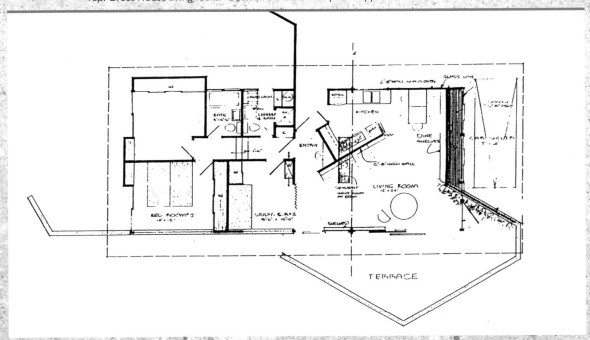

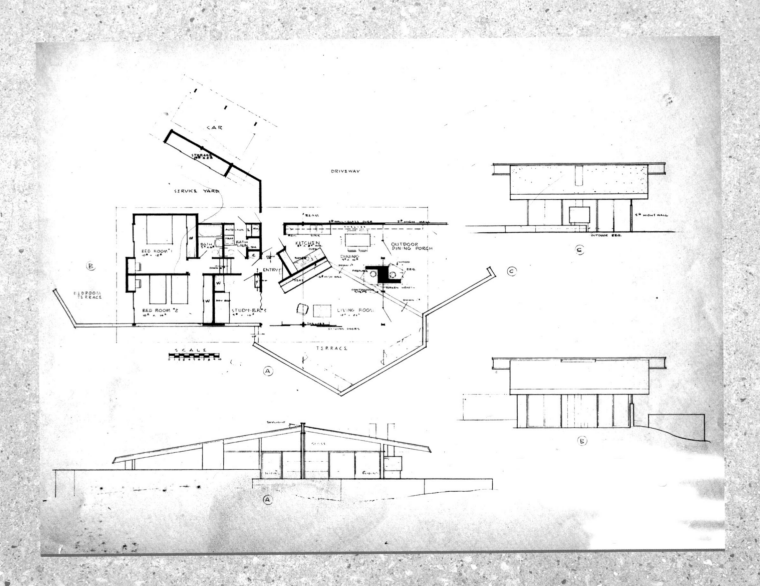

MHA 11X floor plan and elevations

MHA 111X
(2 bedrooms, 2 bathrooms, 1238 square feet, $12,270)

The MHA design chosen by the most members was MHA model 111X, featuring a majestic low-slung gable roof that appears to float over the plywood-clad structure. The seven-foot-high plywood wall facing the street provides privacy for the occupant, while from the street, sight lines through clerestory windows reveal the sky or landscape beyond.

Wurtele House front elevation

An angled mass of colored concrete masonry units serves as a cantilevered fireplace on the interior and extends to the exterior patio, and the concrete hearth inside continues to the outside, dissolving the boundary of indoor and outdoor space, a theme throughout the house.

The MHA 111X transformed a fairly small footprint into what seemed to be a much larger space. Three different floor levels result in a sense of varying ceiling heights, which adds to the sense of drama and space. The kitchen and dining area are on the first level and the living room and den are on another, lower level. The lowest level houses the bedrooms and bathrooms.

Unlike the Pilot House or the Site Office, the posts and beams on the MHA 111X are built-up with a hollow core to house electrical conduit. Such unique detailing added to the beauty of the design but also added to the cost, much to the chagrin of the two contractors who went bankrupt building the first houses, most of them MHA 111X.

Wurtele House // Restoration and alterations: Cory Buckner, Architect
Volk House // Restoration: Cory Buckner, Architect
Haas House // Restoration: Cory Buckner, Architect

Wurtele House living room

Wurtele House view towards living room

Top: Haas House entrance · *Bottom*: Haas House living room

Top left: Volk House kitchen · *Top right*: Volk House hallway
Bottom: Volk House view from living room towards dining room

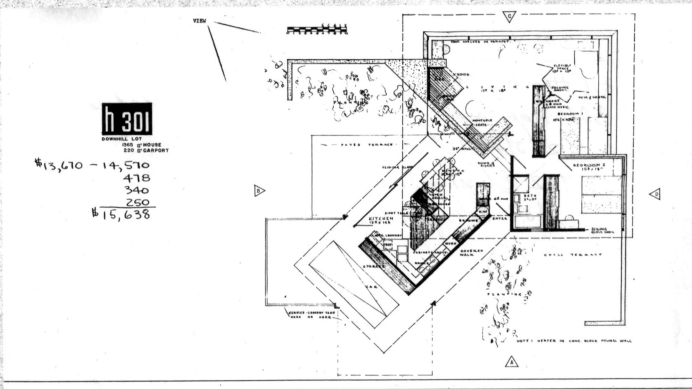

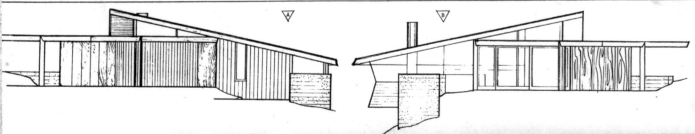

MHA 301 floor plan and elevation

MHA 301
(2 bedrooms, 1 bathroom, 1638 square feet, $15,638)

One of the most dynamic plans originally created is the MHA model 301, which is similar to the MHA 302, it features a roof ridge diagonal to the primarily square plan. A bedroom wing intersects the square at a 45-degree angle.

Designed for a hillside lot to take advantage of the ocean and city light views, the MHA 301 features walls of canted glass that span the entire length of the main living level. The canted glass cuts down on the interior reflections at night, emphasizing the view beyond.

At 1638 square feet, it is also one of the largest of the original designs. The Schneidman family built MHA 301, one of the early houses built. Most MHA 301 houses cost between twelve and fifteen thousand dollars but the Schneidmans included additional living quarters facing the street, which resulted in a final construction cost of $17,588. Madeleine Schneidman lived in the house until her death in 2010.

Schneidman House // Restoration by owners Alex and Kristin MacDowell with consultant Cory Buckner, Architect

Schneidman House entrance

Schneidman House front elevation · *Opposite:* Schneidman House living room

Top: Schneidman House kitchen · *Bottom:* Schneidman House study · *Opposite:* Schneidman House dining room

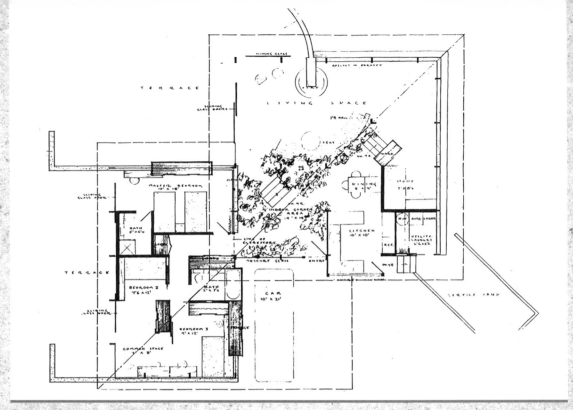

Top: MHA 302 floor plan · *Bottom left:* Kermin House lower floor · *Bottom right:* Kermin House entry

MHA 302
(3 bedrooms, 2 bathrooms, 1723 square feet, $20,096)

MHA model 302 differs from the MHA 301 in placement of the kitchen within the predominantly square plan. The rectangular bedroom wing is placed adjacent to the primary square.

The original owners were Rosalyn and Henry Kermin, Henry being one of four brothers who bought into MHA.

Kermin House // Alterations: Cory Buckner, Architect

Kermin House side elevation

MHA 401
(2 bedrooms, 1 bathroom, 1090 square feet, $10,901)

Several families chose MHA model 401, which was well-suited for large, flat lots. The modest square footage of 1090 square feet was also appealing. But very few of this model were ever actually built, and only one remains in the community as of this writing. The open floor plan had built-in seating facing an angled fireplace.

Brite House // Restoration: Joe and Amita Molloy; additions by Koning Eizenberg Architects

Brite House view from living room • *Opposite:* Brite House hallway

Two views of Friedman House kitchen

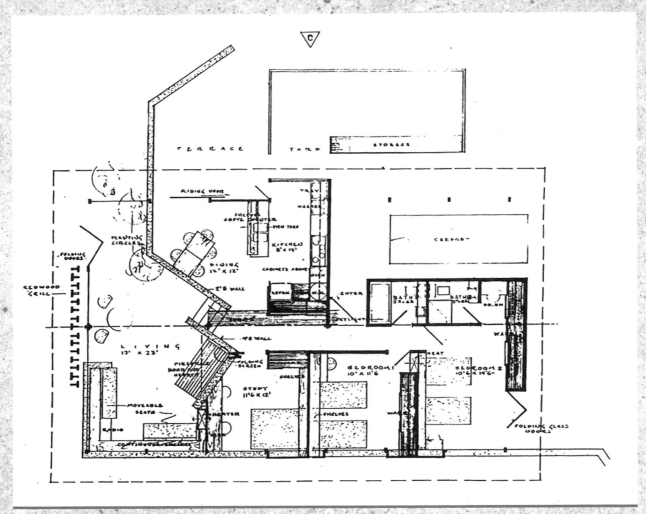

Top: MHA 702 floor plan · Bottom: Elevations

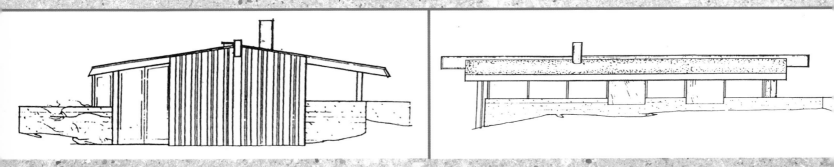

MHA 702

(2 bedrooms, 2 bathrooms, 1350 square feet, $13,867)

The runner-up for most-popular model selected by community members was MHA model 702, designed for a downhill, gently sloping lot. The 1350-square-foot house features two levels. The height of the roof ridge is consistent throughout the length of the house, allowing for greater height in the living area as it steps down from the dining and kitchen area. Along the ridge, small clerestory windows that operate by chains provide light and ventilation.

As with the MHA 111X, the post-and-beam system consists of built-up wood members with a cavity for electrical conduits. Distinguishing features include vertical redwood louvers on the exterior west face to cut down on heat from the late afternoon sun. Inside the house, additional vertical movable louvers separate the living room from the upper level study.

Unlike the closed-off kitchen of the MHA111X, a half-wall separates the kitchen from the dining area; a movable glass panel above the wall serves as a pass-through or shuts off the kitchen for more private dining. The original floor plan called for low, angled, concrete masonry walls dividing the dining area from the living area, but all MHA 702 models in the community were built with straight walls.

A powerful player in the development of Crestwood Hills and its surrounding facilities, Hermann Schott and his family lived in a MHA 702, which was originally the model house furnished by the architects. He lived in the house until 1994.

Schott House // Restoration and alterations: Cory Buckner, Architect
Stein House // Restoration and addition: RAC Design Build, Richard A. Cortez

Top: Schott House living room *Bottom*: Schott House rear elevation *Opposite*: Stein House living room

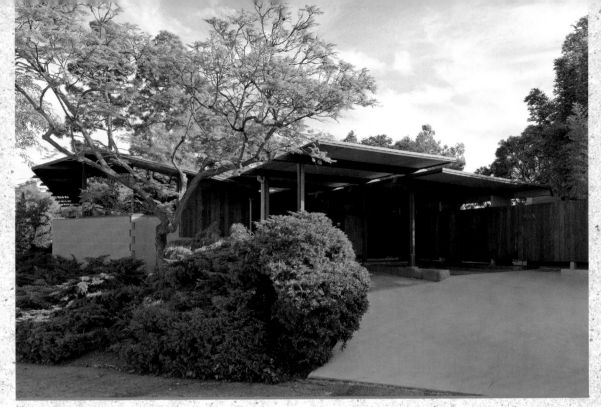

Top: Stein House front entrance · *Bottom*: Stein House view from patio · *Opposite*: Stein House hallway

Top: A. Quincy Jones Steel House front elevation *Bottom:* A. Quincy Jones Steel House living room showing curtains for walls

Zack House

1952 / architect: Craig Ellwood

In 1952, a year after Craig Ellwood had established his design/build company, the architect produced both Case Study House 16 and Zack House. Ellwood stated in the March 1976 article in *L.A. Architect*, "The essence of architecture is the interrelation of mass, space, plane, and line. The purpose of architecture is to enrich the joy and drama of living. The spirit of architecture is its truthfulness to itself; its clarity and logic with respect to its materials and structure." Elegant and serene, situated to take advantage of city lights views, Zack House is the epitome of Ellwood's philosophy. Ellwood went on to build two more houses in Crestwood Hills. The exposed brick privacy wall steps back from the street and is in warm contrast to the stucco walls fronting the street. The rear of the house is transparent, providing canyon views from every major room in the house.

Zack House, view from garden

Top: Johnson House rear elevation · *Bottom*: Johnson House living room

Johnson House

1952 / architect: Craig Ellwood / 3 bedrooms, 2 bathrooms, 1650 square feet, $32,000

Placing the residence horizontally across the slope, Craig Ellwood foreshadowed his later design for Pasadena's Art Center. This axis also provided maximum southwest exposure; with a four-foot overhang and a twelve-inch downturned eave, the living area of the house was protected from the summer sun but heated by the low angle of the winter sun. The bedroom area is protected from afternoon heat gain by vertical louvers.

Ellwood designed the Johnson House with the same eight-foot module and paneled "floating walls" utilized in his contemporary Case Study House #16. The pattern of the structural frame is reflected both in the plan and the vertical elements. Steel posts support wood beams with tongue-and-groove ceiling planks, and interiors are white plaster and natural redwood—a combination of materials that result in a warm livable space. The exterior materials are natural colored plaster and gray-stained redwood. All cabinet work and slab doors are natural finish Philippine mahogany. Steel-framed sliding glass doors open all bedrooms to the dramatic views of city lights and coastline beyond.

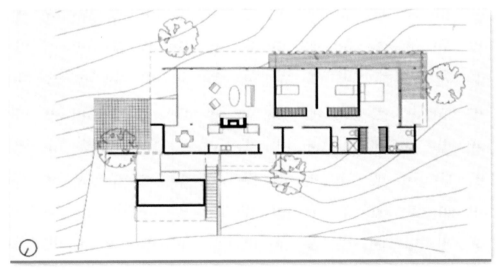

Johnson House floor plan

Johnson House front elevation *Opposite:* Mrs. Johnson on her patio

Knauer House

1954 / architect: Rodney Walker

Rodney Walker began his architecture career as a draftsman for R.M. Schindler in 1938 and spent the war years working as an engineer with Douglas Aircraft. He designed more than one hundred residences in Los Angeles, starting with a house built for his family in West Los Angeles in 1937, followed by Case Study Houses #17 and #18 during the late 1940s.

Knauer House on Bluegrass Lane is one of two houses designed by Walker in Crestwood Hills, and it is the only one extant. It has been altered, but retains the original spirit of the 1954 construction.

Below and opposite: Knauer House lower living area

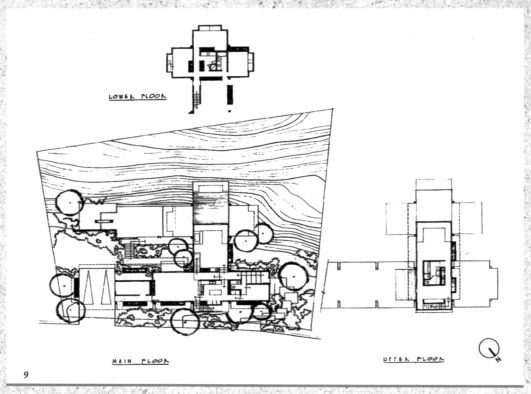

LOWER FLOOR

MAIN FLOOR

UPPER FLOOR

9

Top: Gould House plan · Bottom: Gould House exterior

Gould/LaFetra House
1967 / architect: Ray Kappe

Ray Kappe designed several houses in Crestwood Hills. A major figure in California modernism, Kappe has continued to work in his signature combination of wood, glass, and elegantly organized space. He also was one of the founders of Southern California Institute of Architecture (SCI-Arc). House collector and preservationist Michael LaFetra purchased Kappe's 1967 Gould House on Cloud Lane and engaged the architect as a consultant during the restoration and updating of the house, which now includes an infinity pool and rooftop deck. Perched on a steep hillside, the house appears to float among the trees. At the apex of Canna Road, a cul-de-sac that curls off Tigertail Road, the five-bedroom house embodies Kappe's gentle, organic expression of modernism. Although it is essentially a house of glass, Kappe added warmth with wood: teak, redwood, and mahogany. Douglas fir walls and ceilings complement the built-in furniture and shelving units of the same material.

Gould House model

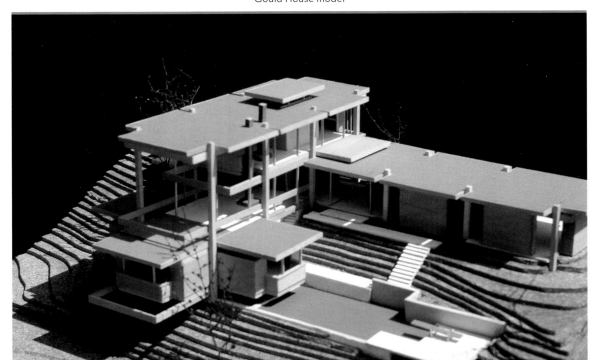

Gale House

1962 / architect: Ray Kappe

MHA model 111X on Lindenwood Lane owned by the Bonderman family, burned to the ground in the Bel Air fire of 1961. Considering the Wrightian influence on the MHA designs, architect Ray Kappe designed a house for new owners of the property, the Gale family. With a variety of pitched roofs and clerestory windows, Gale House is one of two house designs with Wrightian references that Kappe produced during his career: Gale House features wide overhangs and an articulated masonry privacy wall at the street elevation. Like the MHA house designs, the structure consists of exposed posts and beams with exposed tongue-and-groove ceiling planks. The rear of the house is floor-to-ceiling glass revealing the view of Santa Monica Bay in the distance.

Gale House exterior · *Opposite:* Gale House roofline

Shoor House

1952 / architect: William S. Beckett

William S. Beckett graduated from Yale University in 1943 and moved to Southern California to work for Douglas Aircraft a short time during the war. He worked for the firm of Spaulding and Rex from 1944 to 1949, eventually achieving Chief Designer. In late 1949, Beckett went out on his own, and by 1950 he had designed his own office on Melrose Avenue. The Julius Shulman photographs of this building were widely published in the architectural press, winning the AIA National Honor First Award a few years later. This award enhanced his reputation as an architect for stars like Charlton Heston, setting him off on a career designing many celebrity homes and businesses in Beverly Hills and throughout Los Angeles. In 1951, he designed a modest, flat-roofed house on Deerbrook Lane. Construction of the 1000-square-foot Shoor House, with its two small bedrooms and single bathroom, was finished in 1952 for $11,800. The lot is steep; a solid stucco wall fronted the street, while in the back a forty-foot glass wall looked out over the private terrace and canyon below. The glass wall juxtaposed nicely with the solid stucco wall facing the street. The most prominent feature of the interior was a free-standing triangular fireplace that tapered as it rose to the ceiling. Built-in cabinetwork divided the open plan. Once again, Julius Shulman worked his photographic magic. The Shoor House is featured in the 1965 edition of *A Guide to Architecture in Southern California* by David Gebhard and Robert Winter.

Left: Rear of house • *Right*: Living area looking towards view • *Opposite*: Shoor House living room

Adler House

1956 / architect: Richard Neutra

In April of 1955, Dr. Fred Adler, a physicist, commissioned Richard Neutra to design a house for his family on a lot on Kenter Avenue in Crestwood Hills. The 1,870-square-foot house has expansive views of spectacular city lights and Santa Monica Bay. Neutra incorporated his signature ribbon windows facing the view. A steel spider leg in the rear of the house, supports cantilevered beams and roof, which provides shade for the rear garden patio. According to Barbara Lambrecht in *Neutra, Complete Works*:

> But also by this point in his career certain design strategies were standard. "We like the through-going joints to be east and west (thus emphasizing the orientation of the principal long wall) with the staggered joints north and south", he wrote the couple. Despite his reputation for a muted palette he often worked closely with the clients' color preferences, though always channeling them in directions he believed enhanced the overall "integration" of the scheme. Here wall colors were strong yellow, orange, and poppy red, to set odd the natural ash cabinets.

Left: East elevation • *Right:* Street view • *Opposite:* Adler House rear elevation showing spider leg

Sale House

1960 / architect: Richard Neutra

Perched at the top of Tigertail Road, Sale House designed for Robert and Elsa Sale, was built on the level portion of the lot for budgetary reasons. The 2,230-square-foot house features a long gallery for the display of Elsa Sale's art. The gallery with ribbon windows and one wall of the living room with floor-to-ceiling glass face the Pacific coastline view. The primary view in the living room is of the Santa Monica Mountains, since the owner was interested in a woodsy, quiet environment. As with Adler House, a steel spider leg supports a cantilevered roof to the south, providing shade for the living room patio and solar gain protection for the living area. The house was built with sufficient loads to accommodate a second story, which was built at a later date.

Sale House from the hillside above · *Opposite*: Sale House rear with spiderleg

Acknowledgments

Several years ago, London-based photographer John Dooley called me to express an interest in learning more about Crestwood Hills, in hopes of creating a photography book on the neighborhood. Since I was also pursuing my own book project on Crestwood Hills, I suggested we work together, delighted at this extraordinary coincidence. John stayed at our guest house next to the one-time Mutual Housing Association Site Office and spent days carefully creating the majority of the photographs in Part 2. His timing was excellent in terms of the weather and access to the houses; one of houses has been greatly altered since the photo session.

I am especially indebted to Lifetime and interviewer Paula Oliver, who was selected by the Crestwood Hills Association to record oral histories with members who lived and often shaped the Crestwood Hills story. Her 1989 interviews with Art Keyser (September 18), Hermann Schott (September 29), Ray Siegel (September 20), Edgardo Contini (September 29), Myer Bello (October 11), David Schott (October 11), Gerald Tannen (December 6), and Saul Braverman (December 11), were critical to my research, and I have quoted liberally from the interviews she conducted. My thanks also go to Harold Zellman for generously lending me images, suggesting adjustments to the text, and for his thorough research into the Mutual Housing Association. His chapter, *Broadacre in Brentwood The Politics of Architectural Aesthetics*, in *Looking for Los Angeles,* coauthored by Roger Friedland, who was raised in Crestwood Hills, was crucial to my text. I am grateful to Peter Israel and David Schott, both raised in Crestwood Hills, for contributing images and stories of their families and their early days in the community. Original founder, Nora Weckler, as sharp as ever, gave freely of her time, and Harold Meyerson, son of original members Joseph and Estelle, provided an astute political perspective on the community.

I also express my thanks to all the knowledgeable people with whom I have talked over the years and who have helped me understand and appreciate the unique community and history of Crestwood Hills. The Crestwood Hills Archive was invaluable to me.

I would also like to thank Robert Barrett for his brilliant editing, with special thanks to Scott McAuley and Paddy Calistro of Angel City Press for ushering in this publication with superb editing, organization, and humor. Amy Inouye of Future Studio contributed her inventive graphic design, visible on every page of this book.

Cory Buckner
Crestwood Hills, Los Angeles, 2015

Opposite: Sherwood House rear elevation

Photo and Illustration Credits

The author gratefully acknowledges the assistance of these individuals and institutions in assembling and providing illustrations for *Crestwood Hills: The Chronicle of a Modern Utopia.*

Tom Bonner Photography: 121

Brooks Institute students: 12, 97 bottom, 98, 99 bottom, 170

Crestwood Hills Archive: 8, 14-15, 18, 19 bottom, 22, 24, 25, 27, 30, 37 bottom, 39, 40, 41, 44, 45, 46, 47, 49, 50, 51, 52, 53, 54, 56, 57, 58-59, 62, 65, 68, 72, 73, 74, 75, 77 bottom, 78 bottom, 82, 90-91, 97 top, 100, 104, 108, 112, 118 bottom, 120, 126, 132 top, 137, 138, 142, 175

John Dooley Photography: cover, 2-3, 76, 86, 92, 94, 96, 101, 102, 103, 105, 106, 107, 109, 110, 111, 113, 114, 115, 116, 117, 118 top, 119, 122, 123, 124, 125, 127, 128, 129, 130, 131, 132 bottom, 133, 134, 135, 136, 139, 140, 141, 144, 145, 146, 147, 176

Getty Research Institute, Julius Shulman Archive: 5, 6, 10, 34, 35, 60, 64, 69, 70, 71, 78 top, 79, 80 left, 148, 150 bottom, 152 bottom, 153, 158, 159, 164, 165, 166, 167, 168, 169

Darcy Hemley: back flap

Hollywoodphotographs.com: 16

Ray Kappe: 160, 161, 162, 163

National Board of Fire Underwriters: 85

Claudia Otten: 99 top

Marvin Rand: 149, 154, 156, 157

M. Roy Cartography and Design: 88-89

Garrett Eckbo Collection, Environmental Design Archives, University of California, Berkeley: 9, 28

UCLA Special Collections, A. Quincy Jones Archive: 36, 37 top, 150 top

Architecture and Design Collection, Art Design & Architecture Museum, University of California, Santa Barbara: 48

Frank Lloyd Wright Foundation: 32 top, 33, 42

The author also acknowledges the following publications (noted in the bibliography), from whose pages images were sourced:

Arts & Architecture, September 1948: 80 right

Builders' Homes for Better Living by A. Quincy Jones and Frederick E. Emmons: 66, 67

California Modern: The Architecture of Craig Ellwood by Neil Jackson, for the plans by Susan Robertson and Peter Wood: 152 top, 155

"Broadacre in Brentwood" by Roger Friedland and Harold Zellman, *The Getty Bulletin,* Volume 10, Number 2, Winter 1997: 32 bottom, 43

Landscape for Living by Garrett Eckbo: 81

The Living City by Frank Lloyd Wright, Horizon Press, 1958: 19 top

Tomorrow's House, How to Plan Your Post-war Home Now by George Nelson and Henry Wright: 38

John Dooley is a photojournalist and architectural photographer currently based in the UK.

John was Assistant News Photo Editor at *The Daily Telegraph* newspaper for seven years. He went on to become a freelance photojournalist in the USA for six years. His work has appeared in *The Daily Telegraph, The Independent, The Wall Street Journal, Le Monde* and other international publications.

John currently writes his own monthly column in *Black + White Photography* magazine.

Opposite: John Dooley shooting the Sherwood House

Bibliography

Archives:

Crestwood Hills Association Archive located in Crestwood Hills, Brentwood area of Los Angeles, California. The archive includes the Architectural Guidelines referenced liberally in this book, as well as Mutual Housing Association and Crestwood Hills Association brochures, bulletins, photographs, and minutes of meetings.

Getty Research Institute, Los Angeles, California, Julius Shulman and Ray Kappe Archives

A. Quincy Jones papers (Collection 1692). Library Special Collections, Charles E. Young Research Library, UCLA.

Architecture and Design Collection, Art Design & Architecture Museum, UC Santa Barbara

Garrett Eckbo Collection, Environmental Design Archives, University of California at Berkeley, and Frank Lloyd Wright Foundation

Publications:

Buckner, Cory, and A. Quincy Jones. *A. Quincy Jones.* London: Phaidon, 2002.

Bulletin of the Mutual Housing Association, Inc. 2 (January 25, 1947). Volume 2, No. 1

"Couple Earns Honor." *Brentwood Post,* January 25, 1979.

Danenberg, Elsie N. *Get Your Own Home the Co-operative Way.* New York: Greenberg, 1949.

Ditto, Jerry, Marvin Wax, and Lanning Stern. *Eichler Homes: Design for Living.* San Francisco: Chronicle Books, 1995.

Ellwood, Craig. "What Does Post-Modernism Mean to You?" *L.A. Architect,* March 1976.

"Five Hundred Building Bees." *Los Angeles Times Home Magazine,* May 8, 1948.

Gebhard, David, and Robert Winter. *A Guide to Architecture in Southern California.* Los Angeles: Los Angeles County Museum of Art, 1965.

Herman, Valli. "Gould-LaFetra House Sparkles as an Architectural Gem in Brentwood." *Los Angeles Times,* February 15, 2009.

Hines, Thomas S. *Richard Neutra and the Search for Modern Architecture: A Biography and History.* New York: Oxford University Press, 1982.

Hollywood Citizen-News, December 28, 1946.

Hollywood Citizen-News, June 1, 1950.

Jackson, N., and Craig Ellwood. *California Modern: The Architecture of Craig Ellwood.* New York: Princeton Architectural Press, 2002.

Jones, A. Quincy, and Frederick E. Emmons. *Builders' Homes for Better Living.* New York: Reinhold Pub., 1957.

Lamprecht, Barbara Mac., and Richard Joseph Neutra. *Richard Neutra: Complete Works.* Köln: Taschen, 2000. 385.

McCoy, Esther. *Case Study Houses, 1945-1962.* Los Angeles: Hennessey & Ingalls, 1977. 209.

"Mutual Housing Association." *Arts and Architecture,* September 1948.

Mutual Housing Association, Inc. Los Angeles: Mutual Housing Association, 1947.

Nelson, George, and Henry Wright. *Tomorrow's House, How to Plan Your Post-war Home Now.* New York: Simon and Schuster, 1945.

Pilot House. Los Angeles: Mutual Housing Association, 1948.

"Recreation Center Planned for Kenter Canyon." *Brentwood Bel-Air Piper,* April 1, 1955.

Salas, Charles G., and Michael S. Roth. *Looking for Los Angeles: Architecture, Film, Photography, and the Urban Landscape.* Los Angeles: Getty Research Institute, 2001.

Treib, Marc, and Dorothée Imbert. *Garrett Eckbo: Modern Landscapes for Living.* Berkeley: University of California Press, 1997.

Wright, Frank Lloyd. *The Living City.* New York: Horizon Press, 1958.

Zellman, Harold, and Roger Friedland. "Broadacre in Brentwood? The Politics of Architectural Aesthetics." In *Looking for Los Angeles: Architecture, Film, Photography, and the Urban Landscape,* 171-93. Los Angeles: Getty Research Institute, 2001.

Holiday card from the architects

Published by Angel City Press
2118 Wilshire Blvd. #880, Santa Monica, California 90403
+1.310.395.9982
www.angelcitypress.com

Crestwood Hills:
The Chronicle of a Modern Utopia

Copyright © 2015 by Cory Buckner

Design by Amy Inouye, Future Studio

ISBN-13 978-1-62640-024-5 (print)
ISBN-13 978-1-62640-025-2 (e-book)

Library of Congress Cataloging-in-Publication
Data is available

Printed in Canada

The author in her house, formerly the MHA Site Office